CHRISTOPHOBIA

THE REAL REASON BEHIND HATE-CRIME LEGISLATION

By Tristan Emmanuel

Freedom
Press (Canada) Inc.

Ontario Canada

Published by Christian Freedom Press (Canada) Inc.,
Jordan, Ontario, Canada

Printed in Canada

First Edition

ISBN 0-9732757-1-5

Cover Keith Burton

Dedicated to two very dear friends
and respected Christian activists:
Reverend Royal Hamel and Mrs. Lynne Scime.

Contents

Foreword

Complacent Christian beware. If you thought the gay rights movement was just about "tolerance," and that "discrimination" is anti-scriptural and immoral, think again. This deft, compact book examines the lethal threat to religious liberty posed by the rising demand for special "hate laws" to protect homosexuals. Emmanuel explores the terrible paradox wherein gays, who no longer suffer any measurable discrimination at all, angrily seek to suppress the most basic rights of Christians, who on all sides are openly defamed, deplored, mocked and marginalized. Clearly, calmly and boldly, he explains why Christians must stop apologizing, stop hiding, and stop pretending they can coexist peacefully with the perverse new faith that has seized control of North American culture.

Link Byfield
Citizens Centre for Freedom and Democracy

Preface

This book is about Bill C-250. Before it died on the order paper with the adjournment of Canada's Senate on Nov. 12, 2003, Bill C-250 was known as "an Act to amend the Criminal Code of Canada (hate propaganda)." Actually, to be more precise, this book is about legal oppression. Bill C-250, or whatever the Government of Canada may choose to replace it with in the future, represented the latest legislative initiative to silence moral disapproval of homosexuality. Let me take that one step further. Bill C-250 represented the latest attempt to legally suppress the Christian gospel in Canada. In other words, it was the legal face of a very real problem: Christophobia. That is why this book is called: <u>Christophobia: The Real Reason Behind Hate-Crime Legislation.</u>

If you are a Christian concerned about the homosexual agenda, if you are a vocal Christian and you've spoken out in the past because you are deeply concerned about what is happening to our culture, or if you have children who are being raised with a Christian world and life view, then this book is for you. You need to read it. You need to get acquainted with the arguments in this book. You may not agree with everything I say. That is fine. What is important is that you get involved now before we lose any more cultural ground.

A word of caution, however. This book is not for the faint of heart. It is not politically correct. If you're more concerned with appearances or being nice than you are about promoting the truth, and if you worry that you might find some things in this book that would "sound harsh", you are probably not ready for this book. I suggest you get a copy and give it to someone else. Don't get me wrong. This book doesn't go out of its way to insult anyone. But if politically correct niceties concern you more than the hellish condition into which our society has degenerated, then this book is not for you—yet.

This book is my tribute to all those who have fought for the Faith. People like Scott Brockie, a Toronto printer, who was persecuted because he would not print material for the Lesbian and Gay Archives. Hugh Owens, whom I have never met but whose example inspired me to act up, speak up and keep on speaking up.

It was Hugh Owens who, in 1997, decided that he had had enough of the unfettered promotion of the homosexual lifestyle in Saskatoon, Saskatchewan. So, on June 30, in the middle of the city's "Gay Pride Week", he bought advertising space in the local newspaper, the *Star Phoenix*, and ran an ad that presented the other side of the discussion about homosexuality, the side of historic Christianity.

His story is of particular interest to me because of what it means for all of us. Hugh Owens didn't get a discounted rate from the newspaper to run his ad. He didn't raise the money from numerous religious or activist groups, and he certainly didn't get a government grant from the City of Saskatoon, the Province of Saskatchewan, or the federal government. Mr. Owens paid for the ad out of his own pocket.

Why? Because he felt that someone had to say something about the harm homosexuality represents. Someone had to balance the message. It was, after all, "Gay Pride Week" when he ran his ad, and promoting homosexuality was the main agenda (at least in the public media).

But he also did it because it was his constitutional right to express his opinion in the public medium of the day—the local newspaper. He assumed, as any reasonable person would, that if homosexuals could parade their "lifestyle" on the public streets of Saskatchewan's second largest city with government approval and even government funding, that he should not be denied his turn to present the other side.

The ad quoted four Bible references. Following those Bible references was the mathematical equal sign. Behind that was a pencil drawing of two "stick figure men" holding hands. That illustration was enclosed in a circle with a slash through it (the universal "prohibition" sign). The message was clear: the Bible condemns homosexual behavior.

His ad was effective. Perhaps more effective than he wished. Three homosexual activists submitted complaints to the Saskatchewan Human Rights Commission, saying Mr. Owens' ad caused them considerable grief. In fact, the activists argued they should be entitled to compensation for their hurt feelings.

The sole adjudicator from the Saskatchewan Human Rights Commission agreed with the complainants. Ms. Valerie Watson ruled that although Mr. Owens was "publicly expressing his honestly held religious belief as it related to his interpretation of the Bible and its discussion of homosexuality," some "limits" had to be placed on Mr. Owens' right to promote his faith. She said that the Saskatchewan Human Rights Code contained a "reasonable restriction on Mr. Owens' right to freedom of expression." Why? Because the complainants in the case, in her sincere estimation, were "exposed to hatred (and) ridicule (and because) their dignity was affronted on the basis of their sexual orientation."

Ironic, isn't it? Homosexuals flaunt themselves, often in full nudity and sometimes simulating sex acts, at Gay Pride parades across this country and we are supposed to accept it as freedom of expression. And if our dignity is affronted by television images or front-page newspapers shots of these parades, we are told that if we don't like it we should just "not look". Or maybe just look the other way.

It is obvious that equality under the law has become a myth. There are some groups, like homosexuals, who have additional rights that trump the fundamental rights spelled out in the Canadian Charter of Rights and Freedoms. As a result, religious freedom in Canada is now restricted to the right to hold a belief privately. The expression of religious belief is not welcome in the public square, and in the case of Hugh Owens and Scott Brockie, it is forbidden. Courts and tribunals have told Christians (indeed all people of faith) that faith-based speech to address issues of public morality or public policy will be punished.

The message, essentially, is that we are no longer allowed to be "salt" in this world. We had better keep our lamps hidden under a bowl or a basket. We are not allowed to be a "city on a hill", presenting the implications of our faith in public. (Matt 5:13-16)

Bill C-250, while it was alive, represented the latest effort of activists (including some politicians, bureaucrats, and judges) to stifle debate and shut down moral disapproval of homosexuality. In the process, this law would have criminalized the presentation of the gospel in Canada.

The Real Reason Behind Hate Crime Legislation

If you are a Christian and are concerned about this problem, you need to read this book. In it I will examine a few problems:

1) Christian indifference to Christ's lordship and our culture,
2) navel gazing Christianity that always apologizes for speaking truth,
3) the flaws with Bill C-250 and finally,
4) the reality of Christophobia.

In addition to delineating the problems, I will pose a solution. It is radical but I believe it will work.

You may be wondering why I would waste time and effort on a book about a bill that died in the Senate when Parliament was prorogued. The reason is simple. Bill C-250, or its equivalent, will be back. I am absolutely convinced of it. In the current climate in Canada, indeed in North America, the idea of special protection for homosexuals from "hate crime" is gaining great political currency and favor. Christians need to be taught again how to think about these issues. Many of us have been lulled to sleep by our culture, and don't understand how to respond to these challenges.

More importantly, if and when bills like this become law in Canada or the U.S., we have to understand and confess that human laws can change, because human laws are not absolute. It is never a hopeless situation. Man's laws are never static or immutable. Only God's law is. In our democratic societies in North America, we always have the ballot box. But in order for us to demand change, to intelligently raise these issues in the public square, we have to know what we are talking about. We need to be armed with the facts, and we need good arguments. This book is my attempt to develop those arguments.

But there is a broader issue as well; it is called Christophobia. What is "Christophobia"? You've likely never heard of it before. It's a theological term I coined some years ago to describe the irrational reaction of secular humanists and moral revolutionaries, like pro-abortionists and homosexual activists, towards Christianity in general and toward Christians and *Christ* in particular.

For some time we've lived with the pretense that "principled pluralism" can work. It assumes that different religious worldviews, political ideologies and moral value systems can co-exist peacefully here in North America. We Christians have been big proponents of this view. We have assumed that men, made in the image of God, are generally decent—although there is an ongoing discussion about the innate sinfulness of people which I'm not going to get into here—and that human beings will generally choose to live peaceably with everyone.

We are discovering that we have been wrong. There are some value systems and some religious and political ideologies that cannot coexist. For example, secular humanism, the ideology that produced the so-called "sexual revolution" of the Sixties, is not compatible with Christianity, in that it seeks to eliminate religious influence in the affairs of men. It is increasingly militant, totalitarian, and anti-Christian—characteristics shared by many other religions and ideologies. As a result of that hostility, our society is Christophobic. Bill C-250 (or whatever eventually comes to replace it) is a graphic illustration of this cultural/religious war.

December 2003
Jordan, Ontario

Christian Activism
is Love

In the total expanse of human life there is not a single square inch of which the Christ, who alone is sovereign, does not declare, 'That is mine! – **Abraham Kuyper**

A Christian is an activist. I know that sounds radical, even controversial. But it is true. Politics and faith are two sides of the same coin; living for Christ means you cannot separate politics and faith. I base this notion on Scripture and, on my experiences since I began my personal Christian walk.

Now I know that the word "politics" has very negative connotations for some. They consider it a dirty business engaged in by self-centered people. So why do I insist that Christians must be involved in politics? Perhaps politics is the wrong word. Maybe it's better to speak of "the public square." I believe that the Christian faith influences how we think about issues of public policy. For the sake of convenience, in this book, we will use the word "politics" interchangeably with "public policy". Strictly speaking, politics is a natural development and application of my faith. I absolutely believe that Jesus Christ is the King of kings. And that is, if nothing else, a very political statement.

The early Church was very aware of the political implications of the faith. Early Christians were persecuted for their beliefs. Even the Romans who did the persecuting clearly understood that you can't separate politics from religion – they were explicitly persecuting Christians because those Christians refused to worship Caesar as a god. The Christians would not do this because they had another God-King.

> *These who have turned the world upside down have come here too. Jason has harbored them, and these are all acting contrary to the decrees of Caesar, saying there is another king--Jesus. (Acts 17:6-7)*[1]

Christ's kingship, His sovereignty, and His lordship are not so much theological abstracts for me as they are an everyday reality. His lordship is as obvious to me as the fact that He is the Savior. In fact, I can't separate the two. You see, I came to faith in Christ one night while questioning the meaning of my life. I remember taking a late night walk when I was in my early twenties, trying to make sense of the troubles that were colliding all around me. I remember looking up into the night sky and saying, "Okay, if You are real, prove it!" Suddenly a verse came to my mind: "All authority has been given to me in heaven and on earth." (Matt. 28:18)

I had heard that before, as a youngster in the Lutheran Church where I had grown up. I remembered being taught about the "Great Commission" at Sunday school. But that had been a long time ago, and I was a long way from home. So why on earth would that passage come to my mind then and there, on that moonlit walk that became my search for meaning? I didn't realize it that night but not only did my experience open the doors to the Kingdom, it would also compel me to live my faith out in every area of life. It would be "my passage". You know, the passage that first leads us to Christ?

That night, I realized that Christ was a King who died for me. A *King*. He wasn't just some guy. He wasn't just a good man, not just a great teacher, not even simply *the Savior*. No. Christ, the Son of God, was a King. The King of kings, the King of the whole universe, and He was my King. I can tell you, that fact hit me like a ten-ton-truck. I don't think I've ever recovered.

A Pastor Called To Action

That is why I am a Christian activist. That is also why on June 7, 2003, when I heard that Members of Parliament were going to vote in the House of Commons on a bill that would radically challenge Christ's authority in my country and aggressively attack His gospel, I had to act. There really wasn't a choice. Once again the words of the Great Commission echoed loud and clear: "All authority has been given to me." That was all I needed to know. I had to get involved.

I felt that if I, a pastor, did not defend my Lord's interests here in Canada, if I did not defend the right to freely proclaim the gospel, and if I did not defend the need for homosexuals to hear the gospel, then I would be denying the Gospel of Christ. I would never again be able to hold my own office as a minister of this Gospel in high esteem. You see I believed then, and I still believe today, that Bill C-250 was designed to criminalize the gospel message about homosexuality. I have never been more convinced of *anything*.

In response to the threat that this bill might pass, I organized a town hall meeting in my constituency of Lincoln, not far from Niagara Falls, Ontario. I invited our local MP and two other dear friends, Reverend Royal Hamel and Mrs. Lynne Scime. Together we decided to deal head-on with the issue of Bill C-250. We would begin by educating our local Christian community. We'd tell them about the bill, its serious flaws, and its dangerous implications for freedom. We wanted Christians to band together to oppose the passage of Bill C-250 in the House of Commons. We resolved to do everything we could, democratically, to ensure that the bill would not become law.

But there was one big problem. One town hall meeting wasn't enough. There was just too much work to do. There were too many Christians to educate, motivate, and mobilize. As a result, we embarked on a whirlwind town hall tour of Southern Ontario. We visited more than a dozen different federal ridings and conducted 15 town hall meetings. The basic strategy was to lobby the Christian community to get serious about its faith. Our goal was to urge the Christian community across denominational boundaries to tell their elected officials to represent their views in Ottawa. As a result of that political action, I'm even more convinced that motivating the Christian community is the key to changing our nation.

I believe that Christians of all denominations, can be, and indeed, are called to be, the single most influential group in the Canadian body politic. In other words, I believe that Canada (or any nation for that matter) stands or falls by the Church. It is not civil government, not political parties, not big business, and, thankfully, not the United Nations that matter most. The heart, health and prosperity of a nation, any nation, are rooted in the Church, the people of God. This may make me a religious fanatic. I really don't care. I believe that Christians make or break a nation (II Chron. 7:14, Ps. 33:12, Ps. 144:15). That is why I am spending so much of my time speaking and trying to influence Christians. *If we, as Christians, simply understand our mission and catch the vision, we can turn our nation around. I really believe that!*

Skeptics have told me, "There are too few of us to make a difference!" This invariably reminds me of God's words to Abraham as they both looked out over Sodom, "I will spare the city for the sake of ten righteous." (Gen. 18:32)

The Real Reason Behind Hate Crime Legislation

Amazing isn't it? The mere presence of ten righteous people would have averted God's wrath. Listen. I believe that if we stand together, if Christians unite on the core social issues of the day, no democratic society will be able to resist our influence.

In fact, the word of God promises that the Church will ultimately prevail. The Church is unstoppable. The power of Christ, and the reality of the Holy Spirit in every Christian, ensures that the Church will not be thwarted by the forces of wickedness. "And I also say to you that you are Peter, and on this rock I will build my church, *and the gates of Hades shall not prevail against it*. (Emphasis added -- Matt. 16:18-19)[2]

Ask yourself this. If the "gay" population, which only stands at two or three percent of the total population, has had such an impact on society, how on earth can Christians, who comprise about 20%, not do the same? In other words, even if we are not the "moral majority" we can have as much impact as homosexuals have had. But to change our society into one that recognizes the Lordship of Christ, Christians must first be educated, then motivated, *and then they must act.*

This book is my attempt to start to educate Christians in Canada. Canadian Christians are not the only ones wrestling with these social issues. This particular issue, hate crime legislation, transcends national borders, especially in North America. The arguments presented in this book apply equally on both sides of the border. In fact, the new social trends in Canada—hate crime legislation as epitomized in Bill C-250 and the issue of "same-sex marriage"—are major issues in the United States as well. Unfortunately, Canadian courts and legislation have often provided the precedents for initiatives in the United States.

For example, the September 2003 U.S. Supreme Court ruling on the Texas law against sodomy came 36 years after the Canadian one. Canada eliminated anti-sodomy laws when Pierre Trudeau was Justice minister in 1969. The Massachusetts ruling in November 2003, requiring the State to rewrite its marriage laws to allow for "same sex weddings" came just months after similar rulings in the Canadian provinces of Ontario and British Columbia. In fact, the Massachusetts decision cited and concurred with the Ontario decision. (Incidentally all three rulings cited similar grounds, used the same kind of language, and were characterized by an identical subservience to the overriding principles of "human rights", "dignity" and "equality".)

Canada lags behind the USA in most endeavors, from sports to business innovation, to military development and information technology. But, sadly, we've taken the lead when it comes to politically correct initiatives and social engineering.

What Was Bill C-250?

To really understand what this discussion is about, one must know what Bill C-250 said. It was the first legislation of its kind on this side of the Atlantic. Bill C-250 was a "private members' bill". That means, according to the rules of the Canadian Parliament, that this bill was brought forward by a member of parliament, and not sponsored by the governing party. In fact, the private member who proposed it is an avowed homosexual MP, Svend Robinson, a member of the New Democratic Party of Canada from Burnaby, British Columbia. The bill was another step in Mr. Robinson's crusade to get the Canadian government to sanction homosexual behavior. Mr. Robinson has staked a large part of his political career on homosexual rights. (If you're an American, think of Barney Frank. Svend Robinson is sort of a Canadian version of the Massachusetts Congressman. Both men throughout their careers have tried to turn their homosexuality into a political issue by advocating for so-called "gay rights".)

The Real Reason Behind Hate Crime Legislation

Bill C-250 would have amended the *Criminal Code of Canada* by inserting the phrase "sexual orientation" into sections 318 (a section that deals with hate propaganda) and 319 (a section of the code that deals with genocide). Both sections identify categories of people who need protection from the aforementioned "hate propaganda" and "genocide". The current law includes race, ethnicity, and religion as categories that are considered "protected." Mr. Robinson's bill would have added "sexual orientation" to the list of protected categories.

Svend Robinson has argued that his bill was absolutely necessary for the protection of homosexuals from hate-mongers like America's Fred Phelps. He seems to believe that Mr. Phelps is only one of many would-be hate-mongers who hide under the mantle of religion. Homosexuals, according to Mr. Robinson, are routinely discriminated against, intimidated, threatened, and assaulted as a result of the critical commentary by right-wing religious fanatics. All that homosexuals really want, according to him, is to live in peaceful co-existence with everyone else. According to his thinking, this bill would have ensured this peaceful coexistence.

I disagree. First of all, I don't believe the hype about "hate crimes." I don't believe that there are a lot of would-be hate-mongers hiding under the garb of religion. I certainly don't believe that Bill C-250 was about protecting homosexuals. No. I think this bill would have seriously compromised our constitutional freedoms of speech, religion and assembly. (And yes, those values are protected equally in both the Canadian *and* American Constitutions.) Essentially, I'm arguing that this bill was not what it claimed to be and that any similar bill that may be introduced in the future will be just as dangerous. The problem with "hate crime legislation" is the faulty assumptions upon which this kind of law is based, both in Canada and the USA.

I believe, and will attempt to prove to you, that *any* "hate crime law" is really just a front, a Trojan horse, if you will. It will lead to an aggressive attack on Christianity, the gospel, and the Christian ideal of (heterosexual) marriage. The bill will be used to shut down any legitimate criticism of the homosexual lifestyle. That is why I am speaking up. Someone needs to defend the Faith.

So, while I've spoken of being an activist, please understand that my activism is characterized by an absolute concern for the gospel, the Church and Christian marriage. Just as government should create an environment that encourages the development of the free market, it should also create an environment that encourages the free proclamation of the gospel, the building of Churches, and the sanction of Christian marriage and family life. Why? Because government serves a higher purpose than itself. It was created to serve God (Rom. 13:1-4)[3]. But that is a topic for another book.

I should address one very important matter before we move on. Since I began holding public meetings, speaking in churches, and speaking to journalists, some very well meaning Christians have questioned the connection I've made between the gospel and hate crime law. They ask why I think this kind of law would restrict our ability to share the gospel. "After all", they say, "isn't 'religion' another protected category in the Criminal Code? Isn't this bill really just about condemning 'hatred'? What could possibly be wrong with that? Christians are against hate too!"

A Time For Christian Discernment

Now there are two things I find very interesting about these questions. When I hear well intentioned and ostensibly sincere Christians make such statements, the first thing that comes to mind is that the secular media has done a tremendous snow job on the Canadian public. The national media, abetted by others sympathetic to "gay rights," have very successfully spun the truth about hate crime legislation. Lamentably, far too many Christians have been taking their cue from the secular media.

Think about it this way. Where did you first hear about Bill C-250? Was it from the secular media? Not likely. You probably had never heard of the bill until another concerned and informed Christian told you about it. Right? Canada's national media said very little about the bill. I denounced this conspiracy of silence in early 2002 in a piece I wrote for the *Citizen's Report Magazine* (formerly *Alberta Report*). Even when the bill passed in the House of Commons, the media gave it scant attention. And when it died in the Senate? Again, hardly a word was said or written. Throughout the process, most of the coverage in the mainstream media focused on the sympathetic notion that this was a "necessary step in the advancement of 'human rights.'"

Now, the fact that you probably were unaware of Bill C-250 until a fellow Christian brought it to your attention isn't necessarily your fault. After all, we can't all be expected to know everything. But how many Christians tend to view what their brothers and sisters warn them about with skeptical eyes? How often have you said: "I never heard about this before?" Or how about, "Yeah, but the paper told me not to worry about this bill?" The point is that we Christians tend to trust our media more than we trust our fellow believer. Granted, not every Christian is informed. Granted, some over-react. But we have a responsibility to consider seriously the information we get from our brothers and sisters. This is especially true when the secular media is routinely silent on issues that matter to Christians.

My second reaction to doubting Christians is even more distressing. I wonder, "Have we sold out?" In my encounters with many Christians over the years I have reluctantly concluded that modern culture has so permeated the lives of Christians that they just don't get it. Perhaps they don't even want to get it. Christ's kingship should be abundantly obvious to every Christian. Sadly it is not. Nothing makes this more apparent than the way Christians reacted, or failed to react, to Bill C-250.

Too many Christians believe that hate crime law for homosexuals and "same-sex marriage" are an inevitable and even progressive development of human rights. Ostensibly sincere Christians have told me, "Gays have rights, irrespective of what we believe about their sexual behavior." These same "believers" are convinced that the mark of genuine Christianity is in loving them, by which some of them mean total acceptance and tolerance of their behavior. Besides, they say, if we come across too strong on this issue we'll look judgmental. We'll "scare them off", and no one wants that, right? Finally, if we oppose "gay rights," these same Christians suspect (and sometimes accuse) us of hate mongering, that is, doing the very thing Bill C-250 was supposed to prevent.

Let me cite, as an example, Reverend Troy Perry, a "minister" from the U.S., who was quoted in an Ontario seniors' paper, Forever Young. Rev. Perry was commenting on David Mainse's mission to save marriage. Notice his hostility to traditional Christian values:

> *I have heard the majority say this about minorities throughout history. . . In my own culture the Ku Klux Klan said we don't really hate black folks, we just don't want them to go to school with our children. Black birds and blue birds don't rest in the same nest. I've heard all these arguments before. Hate, whatever you dress it up as, is still hate.* [4]

Now, perhaps you're thinking that Rev. Perry is from the liberal wing of the Church and that I'm just pulling out gratuitous quotes to make my point. Well, he is a liberal. There is no denying that. In fact, the seniors' paper was a little misleading. Rev. Perry isn't simply a member of the clergy (and I'm not really sure he is legitimately ordained). He is the self-appointed founder of the Metropolitan Community Church—a worldwide pro-homosexual "church" he started in 1968, to support gays, lesbians, bisexuals, and transgender persons. That makes him one of the leading gay activists in the United States of America today. Why did the seniors' paper pass him off as a minister? Perhaps they had a hard time distinguishing between conventional ministers and the gay activist type? On the one hand this seems very misleading, yet on second thought sometime it can be difficult to distinguish them. Many so-called conservative, evangelical pastors and believers are saying and thinking the same things.

Is Indifference Love Or Hate?

Here is why that is. Since the town hall meetings began, a number of Christians have declared that it isn't our place to determine public policy. Christians, they say, just need to be filled with the love of Christ. In fact one pastor suggested to me that it would be unchristian to oppose Bill C-250. I was dumbfounded at first, and didn't know how to respond. I realized, however, that if love is really what motivates Christians, how is it expressed in our actions?

Christian love should be expressed, above all else, as devotion and loyalty to Christ. We should love Him not only as our Savior, but also as our Lord. In addition, we should acknowledge and love the fact that He is the Lord of our nation. Instead, what I've witnessed in some cases is radical indifference.

Here are the facts:
1) If we are motivated by love, then we must be motivated by godly, holy love (Rom. 12:9).
2) Holy love is defined by the first and great commandment: "You shall love the LORD your God with all your heart, with all your soul, and with all your strength" (Deut. 6:5).

3) Loving God means that we should keep his commandments. "If you love me, keep my commandments" (John 14:15).

The last point is particularly relevant to those who claim to be motivated by love. When they say that we should just love homosexual people and not get involved in public policy, they have conceded a very important principle. The notion that public policy is the exclusive domain of the government or the Human Rights Commission, is in direct conflict with our belief in Christ's absolute authority to proscribe the proper limits of human sexuality and human rights. Remember: "*All* authority has been given to me in heaven and on earth." This also means that Christ has the authority to define what a "human right" is.

Christians should get this straight. Jesus Christ, the King of kings, is the One who determines what a human right is. No one else. He and He alone, can do this because "all authority has been given to (Him) in heaven and on earth." Christ isn't speaking only of spiritual authority. He is speaking of every kind of authority. He has the authority to proscribe spiritual truth, economic truth, and yes, political truth, which includes human rights. Christ has authority over *everything*. Moreover, His authority and His truth supersede the authority and dogma of the United Nations, any Human Rights Tribunal, or even that of the Liberal Party of Canada or the Democratic Party in the U.S.

When I hear Christians proclaiming that "homosexuals have rights," and charging that anyone opposed to these "rights" must be "motivated by hate", I cringe. The plain fact is that too many Christians have embraced secular notions on human rights that conflict with their loyalty to Christ. If we are motivated by Christian love, we will want to guard Christ's universal authority over these man-made notions of human rights that conflict with God's law. Christians cannot remain indifferent about Christ's universal authority if they want to effect change, either in Canada or the United States.

The Real Reason Behind Hate Crime Legislation

The LORD brings the counsel of the nations to nothing; He makes the plans of the peoples of no effect. The counsel of the LORD stands forever, the plans of His heart to all generations. Blessed is the nation whose God is the LORD. (Ps. 33:10-12)

There is also the question about truly loving homosexuals. Is love indifferent to the severity of homosexual sin? I think that most people think they love, or are being "loving", simply because they aren't visibly upset about homosexuality. In other words, they don't get too agitated or judgmental about the sin. Homosexuality, they say, is just another sin, and we are all sinners after all, right? But this is confused thinking about the nature of love and hate and the nature of homosexual sin.

Hate manifests itself in many different ways, one of which is indifference. Think of the Good Samaritan. In this parable Christ clearly illustrates that indifference and hatred can be the same thing. The Israelites revealed their hatred for the hurting man at the side of the road, not by beating him, but by refusing to help when he was most in need. It was the Samaritan who showed love, because he cared enough to get involved.

So which of these three do you think was neighbor to him who fell among the thieves?" And he said, 'He who showed mercy on him.' (Luke 10:36-37)

Many Christians talk about love, and yet appear unmoved by a sinful lifestyle that is gaining legal recognition and approval in our society. They don't want to get involved politically in the issue. I wonder if it really isn't indifference, rather than solid conviction, that is causing them to evade their responsibility. I believe that it is hateful to ignore the truth about this issue. It is hateful to misrepresent the seriousness of homosexuality. Are we all sinners? Absolutely. But that misses the point completely. The concern is not about the equality of all sins. The concern is with the unique social consequences that certain sins bring.

Some sins, by their very nature, are more serious and destructive. Homosexuality is one of these sins. It is devastatingly addictive. It involves a lifestyle of misery, enslavement, and violence for many homosexuals who feel absolutely trapped. It subjects people to untold health consequences and sadly, to eternal alienation. The only remedy that can possibly set homosexuals free from this very serious sin is the gospel. If we aren't convinced that the sin of homosexuality is that serious, we probably won't think it that important to share the gospel with them. Once it becomes illegal to do so because of laws like Bill C-250, I wonder if many Christians will even want to bother.

I must stress the power of the gospel. I believe that the gospel is the only hope. Now, in saying this, I am not suggesting that we take no interest in changing social norms. Obviously, as citizens of this democracy, we have an equal interest and right to influence the social norms that governments advocate or discourage. But government is not ultimately the answer, the gospel is. We must always keep that front and center. The gospel alone has the power to change the hearts and minds of men and women. Only the gospel will change homosexuals.

The apostle Paul refers to the gospel as the "power of God"

- *For I am not ashamed of the gospel of Christ, for it is the power of God to salvation for everyone who believes, for the Jew first and also for the Greek. (Rom. 1:16)*

- *For the message of the cross is foolishness to those who are perishing, but to us who are being saved it is the power of God. (1 Cor. 1:18)*

Through the gospel God doesn't simply redeem man from the debt of sin and the torment of hell. By the gospel God changes human lives. The gospel is life. It is God's power to regenerate all those dead in their trespasses and sins. All those spiritually dead and under the dominion of Satan, receive life through the gospel. Again, Paul writes:

The Real Reason Behind Hate Crime Legislation

And you He made alive, who were dead in trespasses and sins, in which you once walked according to the course of this world, according to the prince of the power of the air, the spirit who now works in the sons of disobedience, among whom also we all once conducted ourselves in the lusts of our flesh, fulfilling the desires of the flesh and of the mind, and were by nature children of wrath, just as the others. But God, who is rich in mercy, because of His great love with which He loved us, even when we were dead in trespasses, made us alive together with Christ … (Eph. 2:1-5)

The gospel is the most powerful message in the history of mankind. It is grounded in Divine love. It is, and will always remain, our only hope.

Now, I think that many Christians understand this. I'm sure that most Christians believe it. But I'm not so sure that many have considered how powerful an apologetic the gospel really is. The gospel is the single greatest argument against the secular doctrine of genetic homosexuality. The argument that homosexual activists offer to oppose the gospel is really futile if you think about.

What do I mean? Homosexual activists are trying to establish that homosexuality is biologically determined so that they can neutralize the ethical and religious objections. They think that if they can prove homosexuality is natural, that they were born that way or even made that way by God then there is nothing wrong with homosexual lust or behavior and consequently no need to change.

But herein lies their glaring error. To establish that something is biologically "natural" (which has not been conclusively done with homosexuality, and I suspect never will be), still does not vindicate the behavior. That is to say, just because someone was "made that way", doesn't mean that he or she should "stay that way". Christians should understand that original sin brought about a host of original complications. Even if science were to discover the so-called "gay gene," and categorically determine that homosexuality is a genetically determined condition, this "discovery" would still not override or refute the gospel. If the gospel, which is the power of God, can redeem sinners from hell, if it can recreate life from spiritual death, then it is also powerful enough to change our temporal existence here on earth. In other words it can change our lifestyle.

When Adam and Eve fell from grace, the Scripture tells us that all of creation was subjected to the "curse." (Rom. 8:19-22) As a result, all people became subject to the miserable conditions and consequences of sin. From the standpoint of biology, this means that biological irregularities, like inbred and inherent disabilities, human diseases, and other aberrations are part and parcel of the human experience. In some sense, biological irregularities that contribute to the misery of the human life are "natural," but they are certainly not desirable.

I say this simply to point out that there is no great threat to our position from medical science. We do not need to worry that the discovery of a "gay-gene" will nullify the ethical imperatives to live sexually pure lives or the claims of the gospel to change and redeem men and women from the miseries of homosexual sin. The gospel is the power of God to change human life. The gospel alone can lift man out of the muck and mire, the misery, the unwanted biological urges and desires of humanity, and lift him to a plane that he could never naturally attain.

> *This I say, therefore, and testify in the Lord, that you should no longer walk as the rest of the Gentiles walk, in the futility of their mind, having their understanding darkened, being alienated from the life of God, because of the ignorance that is in them, because of the hardening of their heart; who, being past feeling, have given themselves over to lewdness, to work all uncleanness with greediness. But you have not so learned Christ, if indeed you have heard Him and have been taught by Him, as the truth is in Jesus: that you put off, concerning your former*

conduct, the old man which grows corrupt according to the deceitful lusts, and be renewed in the spirit of your mind, and that you put on the new man which was created according to God, in true righteousness and holiness. (Eph. 4:17-24)

This is why the gospel is so important and why we Christians need to defend it against aggressors who seek to suppress it.

There is one last important point about love. If we are truly motivated by love then we cannot ignore the implications that hate crime legislation and "same-sex marriage" will have on future generations. If we are truly motivated by love we have no choice but to oppose the homosexualization of our culture. We must decry it because it condemns future generations, including our children and grandchildren, to unspeakable national judgment. History is replete with examples of civilizations coming under the direct judgment of God because of sexual perversion. Lest we think that every judgment needs to be as dramatic as Sodom, divine judgment can also take a slower and more long-suffering form. In the case of Rome, for example it took several hundred years before the Barbarians invaded and completely dismantled that empire. But the cracks had begun to appear from within, as Rome became increasingly corrupt and perverse, making the Empire easy prey for the Barbarian conquest.

Of course, many Christians are convinced that we are actually in the last days right now. That may or may not be. Jesus repeatedly warned, "of that day and hour no man knows... (Matt. 24:36) It is not in our best interest to be consumed with the question of Christ's imminent return, especially if that distracts us from doing what He commissioned us to do in the first place. If Jesus is returning soon, then we should make sure that He returns to find us busy doing kingdom work, and kingdom work involves social action. Let's let Him determine the year, month, day and hour of his return. We do our duty and let God take care of hour of Christ's return. It was the reformer Martin Luther who said, correctly that, "if I knew Christ was coming back tomorrow, I would plant a tree today." As Christians, we are called to be busy with the work the Lord has placed before us irrespective of where we are on the historical timeline leading up to the second coming of Christ.

The opposite of love is hate.   And hate is *characterized* as indifference. Indifference is hateful because we are commanded to "love . . . without hypocrisy. Abhor what is evil. Cling to what is good." (Rom.12: 9) If we say that we are motivated by love, and yet we turn a blind eye to evil masquerading as a fundamental "human right," we are not only betraying our loyalty to Christ, we are also betraying homosexuals. We are also betraying the next generation of Canadians and Americans.   Surely Christian love cannot and should not be this hypocritical!

2

Stop Being Defensive

Liberals don't try to win arguments, they seek to destroy their opponents and silence dissident opinions.—
Ann Coulter

I apologize for linking the homosexual community with pedophilia. I was wrong to draw such an inference. I apologize to my colleague Svend Robinson. I have the utmost respect for Mr. Robinson as both an individual and as a parliamentarian.—**Larry Spencer, MP**

On September 17, 2003, I gathered with a group of clergy to respond to the passage of Bill C-250 in the House of Commons. We wanted to urge the Canadian Senate to give sober second thought to the bill. In addressing the Senate and the national press, we gave the following as our opening statement:

> *We preface our statement by saying that as clergy we are motivated by Christian love. As ministers of the Gospel of Peace, we feel it is important to constantly re-affirm this axiom, particularly because of the highly contentious nature of Bill C-250, and because of the general climate of politically correct speech. As ministers of the Gospel we re-affirm our love for*

homosexual persons, though we morally disapprove of homosexual sexual practices. It is love, love for our nation and love for homosexual persons that causes us to stand here and challenge the legitimacy of Bill C-250.

Since that press conference, I've noticed a number of other organizations make similar statements. For example, I recently came across this one: "[We] do not condone nor support the promotion of hatred or acts of violence towards any person, nor do we condone speech that incites people to violent acts."

Both statements are examples of what is commonly called a "disclaimer." A disclaimer is a statement that renounces the opinion or action of another group. It creates legal separation. You've probably seen broadcasters issue these kinds of statements whenever a religious or political program is aired. Broadcasters want to ensure that no one will associate them specifically with the views expressed on those programs. A disclaimer is issued to avoid confusing the viewing or listening audience.

The same goes for us. We want to ensure that no one associates Christians who are speaking out against this hate crime law with actual hate-mongers. No self-respecting Christian person or organization condones or supports the proliferation of hatred. However, having thought the issue through, I have come to the conclusion that when we go out of our way to issue disclaimers like the one mentioned above, we might be doing more harm than good.

The fact that Christian organizations feel it necessary to restate the obvious demonstrates that there are inherent flaws in our politically correct culture. If we are going to defend freedom of speech and freedom of religion, and if we are going to advance the truth and promote the gospel, we must not only expose the flaws of politically correct speech, but also contend with and reverse the secular standards of public discourse. If we do not do this, not only will we lose the present battles, we will lose the culture war.

There are several reasons why the "we-do-not-condone-hate" disclaimer is not only unnecessary, but also counterproductive to what we are trying to accomplish.

Why Do We Repeatedly State The Obvious?

First, all such disclaimers are superfluous. Of course, no reasonable and responsible person or group condones or supports the promotion of hatred. Respect, benevolence and charity are the assumed positions of anyone who cherishes freedom, democracy and the advancement of peace in a nation. Christians, of all people, cherish and uphold all three.

Now, restating the obvious isn't always wrong. But it can be unnecessarily redundant. If we have to restate these obvious truths every time we address the issue of homosexuality, it means one of two things. Either Christians have done a very poor job of communicating their love for democracy and an orderly and peaceful society, or the average citizen hasn't the faintest idea what a Christian really is. I suspect both of these things are true to one extent or the other. Nevertheless, if we continue to restate the obvious whenever we speak, we will be viewed as nothing more than "politically correct".

Politically Correct Standards Are Man's, Not God's

Our politically correct environment has created a double standard, and a disclaimer advances those views. The unwritten rule of public discourse in North America today is that anything written or stated publicly from a conservative Christian perspective has to be done softly and in a moderate tone. It has to give credence to "diversity" and bow at the altar of "tolerance." If our writing or public statements do not live up to these rules, we are immediately condemned as judgmental, bigoted, and promoters of harsh hate speech.

However, the same standard is not applied to those who are critical of historic conservative Christianity. You'll be hard pressed to find any homo-sympathetic organization give a similar disclaimer about how "We don't hate Christians, nor do we encourage violence against Christians, etc . . ." when they raise objections. In fact, it is the exact opposite. Homo-sympathetic persons and groups don't moderate their vitriol at all. They don't preach a diversity that includes conservative Christianity, and they are absolutely *intolerant* of historic Christian virtues, values and morality. In most cases, they use exaggerated rhetoric to castigate the "religious right" as hate-mongers but they never produce the evidence to back up the claim. So, who is kidding whom?

The double standard is so ingrained that national media outlets are not faintly worried that they will be held accountable for flagrant and slanderous accusations against Christians. For example, in discussing the murder of Matthew Shepard, a gay man brutally killed by two men in Wyoming, Deborah Mathis of Garnet News Service explained:

> *The Christian right per se . . . have helped inflame the air so that the air that those people breathed that night was filled; filled with the idea that somehow gays are different, and not only are they different, but in there (sic) difference they're bad, and not only are they bad, they are evil, and therefore can be destroyed . . . I mentioned . . . the Christian Coalition, the Family Research Council and the Concerned Women for America...*

Christians were responsible for poisoning the air that the thugs breathed? Therefore *Christians* are the cause of Matthew Shepard's murder? Her comments are beyond outrageous. They are malicious and slanderous. But who will hold her accountable? The secular media? She is part of the secular media. Even more outrageous, is knowing that if the shoe were on the other foot Christians would never get away with this kind of rhetoric. For example, what if we were to argue that homosexual activists "inflamed the air Matthew breathed" because they promoted seedy homosexuality that put Matthew Shepard directly in touch with vicious masochistic murderers? If we said that, we'd be hauled off to the nearest human rights tribunal.

Like it or not, there is a double standard. Our "disclaimers" only perpetuate that double standard. Instead of holding slanderers in the media accountable for violating their own rules, we are more concerned with being rhetorically and politically correct, and making sure everyone sees that we are.

Where Is All The Hate Anyway?

Furthermore, and most importantly, a disclaimer reinforces the wrong message. When our public statements continually include reminders that we reject all forms of hate crime we directly, whether we realize or not, reinforce the idea that there is in fact an epidemic of hate crime being perpetrated against homosexuals. This is simply false (Chapter four will explain this all in greater detail.). The fact is that there is no epidemic of hate crime against homosexuals. Homosexuals are not victims. Some may have been victimized, but this is no more or less true of them than it is of any other group in our society.

The rallying cry of "hate crime" is simply propaganda that homo-sympathetic people and organizations have used to break down natural barriers. As one of their own stated, "(to get) straight America to accept us we need to be seen as victims."[5]   When we issue a disclaimer, we are participating in that strategy. We are spreading their propaganda by perpetuating the lie that homosexuals are daily subjected to great crimes of hate.

The facts show something completely different. Statistical data related to hate crime against homosexuals is negligible in both Canada and the USA. That doesn't mean that homosexuals don't experience crime against their person or property. It just means that there is no epidemic. Furthermore, whatever crime is being carried out against them it does not rise to the level of mass persecution–nothing comparable for example to the Jewish Holocaust in Nazi Germany—and therefore there is no justification for creating a special law that singles out homosexuals for protection.

Moreover, whatever statistical data does exist does not distinguish carefully between hate crime against homosexuals by people with traditional and religious views, and those committed by gays against gays. The facts speak for themselves. Homosexual authors David Island and Patrick Letellier in their book, _Men Who Beat the Men Who Love Them_, exposed the extent of gay violence. They estimate that in the United States alone, up to 500,000 gay men are battered by their lovers every year. Yet the pro-gay media won't print the truth about gay-on-gay violence. Island and Letellier, offer this as the excuse:

> [I]t would be just plain bad press for gays [. . . and] all bad news needs to be suppressed. [G]ay men truly have a [disproportionate] share of violent individuals in their midst who bash other gay men [and boys] in startlingly high numbers. The gay community needs to recognize that wealthy, white, educated, 'politically correct' gay men batter their lovers.

We Protest Too Much

Finally, a disclaimer undermines our ultimate point because it raises suspicion about our genuineness. As Shakespeare wrote, "... the lady doth protest too much." If we are not motivated by hate, then why are we on the defensive? Why are we prefacing every talking point, editorial, teaching and sermon with a disclaimer about how we don't condone hate? We certainly don't do this for anything else the Bible judges to be sinful. For example when Christians speak about the sin of "theft" we generally don't preface our comments about how we love the thief. Take smoking as another example. In today's climate it is socially unacceptable. Society disapproves of smoking and speaks very bluntly about the issue. "Smoking is dirty." "Smoking is disgusting!" "Smoking should be banned from public places." In fact some jurisdictions do ban smoking. Now, how often have you heard people preface their disparaging remarks about smoking, or smokers with, "We just want smokers to know that we love them, it is just their behavior we disapprove of... ." You've never heard that. And why is that? Is it because society hates smokers? No. It is because it is simply not necessary. So why do we preface our remarks when speaking about homosexuality? To outsiders listening to us, our disclaimer actually makes us look disingenuous.

The bottom line is this. Christians are to be motivated by Christian love. Anything else is a contradiction and issuing a disclaimer confuses the issue. It is unnecessary and redundant. It propagates politically correct rules, and it fails to confront the secular double standard.

There is nothing wrong or hateful about a Christian publicly opposing a law like Bill C-250. This bill was riddled with flaws—the subject matter of the next few chapters. It was not about protecting homosexuals from mass hatred. Instead, it would have provided a billy club to whack legitimate critics—religious or otherwise—with criminal suits. Bill C-250 was a concerted effort to crush the gospel of Christ. That is why, if we truly are motivated by Christian love, we cannot remain indifferent when the gospel is being attacked. We need to understand why laws like Bill C-250 are fundamentally flawed, and we must aggressively oppose the thinking that underlies them. While we are at it, we need to stop apologizing for speaking the truth.

CHRISTOPHOBIA

3

Why A Hate Law?

There are sections of the Criminal Code that direct the courts to take into consideration if a sentence should be increased or reduced to account for crimes based on someone's sexual orientation... in effect, there is provision for consideration in sentencing for any crime that has been motivated because of someone's sexual orientation. – **Senator Terry Stratton**

The Criminal Code Is Sufficient

I recently attended a meeting of ministers of the gospel, a "Ministerial Association" meeting of pastors from various denominations. The focus of the meeting was "same-sex marriage" and Bill C-250. To my utter chagrin, one evangelical pastor suggested that discrimination against any homosexual is "...untenable, and therefore a Christian should support Bill C-250."

Untenable? What was and is untenable is a law like Bill C-250, and any *pastor* who suggests otherwise needs to rethink the facts. There are reasons why providing special protection for homosexuals in a "hate crime bill" is flawed. Christians need to know these and be able to address them intelligently if we are going to challenge politically correct dogma.

The first flaw in this law is the implication that existing law is insufficient to protect homosexuals from crime. This is simply false.

A law does not provide protection. It never has and it never will. Law is powerless to change a person's heart. It is a great fallacy, but one that social engineers, including the homosexual lobby, have been promoting for years. If law could protect, it would be supernatural, divine, having the ability to change an assailant into a peace-loving person. No, law has ever accomplished this, not even God's law (Rom. 8:3).

A law is a standard of what is right and wrong. It points people to what is socially, culturally, and morally acceptable (Rom. 7:7). It also determines the proper course of action in the event that the law is contravened. But that is all a law does. That's all it can do. And all it *should* do. When homosexuals argue that existing laws don't provide adequate "protection" they are misrepresenting the purpose of law. They are trying to turn "law" into a political savior. They get away with it because most people, even Christians, are ignorant about the purpose of the law.

In fact, the *Criminal Code of Canada*, while it does not protect anyone, does provide adequate legal remedy to deal with crimes against homosexuals, just as it does for crimes against any other Canadian citizen. The charge that existing laws are insufficient is not defensible with facts or good legal arguments. Homosexuals have just as much protection under the *Criminal Code of Canada* as anyone else does.

In fact, Canada's law is so comprehensive that it not only provides legal sanction against those whom actually carry out crimes (like personal assault, theft, and vandalism), but it also provides remedies to prosecute "third party" assailants. Section 22 of the *Criminal Code* makes it a criminal offence to counsel (i.e., teach), procure (i.e., purchase), solicit or incite (i.e., encourage by way of speech or writing) others to commit assaults and/or other offences on any person or property whether or not the offences are actually committed. Notice the phrase **"whether or not the offences are actually committed."** That's pretty comprehensive.

Moreover, hate motivated crime is also dealt with in the *Criminal Code.* Section 718.2 of the Code provides that more "onerous punishments" should be imposed for crimes against person(s) or property that are motivated by "bias, prejudice or hatred based on race, national or ethnic origin, language, color, religion, sex, age, mental or physical disability" and -- you guessed it-- "sexual orientation." The federal Liberal Government added the last part in 1995.

Furthermore, Section 810 of *Criminal Code* gives judges the punitive power to impose a "recognizance of the peace" against anyone found guilty of "counseling hatred" against any person, (that means any speech or writing that encourages or influences others to carry out a criminal act). Again, notice that to be *party to crime by simply directing it,* but not actually committing it, is a crime under the *Criminal Code of Canada.*

Existing law is clearly sufficient to deal with hate crime. In fact, some parts of the Criminal Code verge on being totalitarian. Section 718.2 gives judges the power to judge *emotion.* This is, by explicit Biblical standards, patent nonsense and certainly not the role of the judiciary. The Bible tells us that no man can judge the heart of another man. Only God can judge the heart (1 Cor. 2:11; Jer. 17:10). The reason should be obvious. Issues of the heart are largely elusive to carnal man (Jer. 17:9). Judging the human heart requires omniscience and infallibility, qualities no human judge possesses. But the secular state no longer respects the ontological differences between God and man. It has banished God from the public square, and now rushes in to fill the vacuum. The state wants to be like God and judge (very fallibly, mind you) the hearts of men.

Even though Bill C-250 was unnecessary, its promoters, including the mainstream media, perpetuated fallacies, and some Christians have blindly fallen for this propaganda.

However, pastors, who are charged with the care and feeding of God's flock, have a responsibility to know better. I find it astounding that an evangelical pastor would make the statement that "discrimination against homosexuals is untenable and therefore a Christian should support Bill C-250." Note well that I said I find it astounding. Not surprising, because it's easy to be taken in by the propaganda. This brother may be ignorant of the facts, or he may be sympathetic towards homosexuality. I don't know. I don't pretend to know his heart. But one thing I do know. No pastor has the right to bind the conscience of other Christians where the Word of God has not. That would be untenable.

4

Where Is All The Hate Crime?

Hatred of gays and lesbians has profound and devastating consequences: We all know what kids in schoolyards and playgrounds do when they want to gang up on one of their group. The most efficient and effective attack is to call someone a fag, "la tapette." That immediately destroys the capacity of that young person to be one of the group, to be seen as an equal member of society. — **Senator Serge Joyal**

If listening to an evangelical pastor at the Ministerial meeting extol the virtues of Bill C-250 wasn't bad enough, having the guest speaker (a local politician) condemn any and all discrimination against homosexuality was simply outrageous. Let me quote him directly. "Even one act of discrimination against homosexuals should not be tolerated." Now you may agree with his sentiment, but the problem is this: how did we go from talking about "hate crime" to the undefined and catchall term of "discrimination"?

All of this begs the question; what is it that these people *really* want? Stopping hate crime (whatever that might mean) is one thing, and it might even be a good thing if it were possible (which it is not). It seems, however that the real agenda here is to label any act of "discrimination" as a hate crime.

Discrimination As Christian Virtue

Perhaps you are a little uneasy about defending discrimination. "Oooh, I don't know. Are you saying a Christian *should* discriminate?" It used to be that "discrimination" was a good thing. We spoke of people with "discriminating taste". Evidently, however, if the most popular TV sitcoms can be considered evidence, this kind of discrimination is sadly lacking in society today. (If people truly had "discriminating taste", these sitcoms would not be popular.) Good taste aside, it is a Christian duty to be discriminating. The Scriptures command us to discriminate between right and wrong, good and evil. It teaches us to make judgments. To "test the Spirits." (I John 4:1) In other words, to be "discriminating." In fact as a Christian, if you're not "discriminating" or making a choice, you should be. Particularly when it comes to homosexuality.

For example, I would never allow a homosexual to teach my children. If our politically correct society wants to call that discrimination, so be it. But I would never allow a homosexual to be a role model for my children, or anyone else's children. This has everything to do with how I view life, and God, and the world around us. There are certain values promoted in my home, values I don't want contradicted in school or at Scouts or wherever my children might be influenced. Not to gratuitously equate homosexuality with any heinous crime in particular, but I wouldn't want a thief, a child molester, or an unrepentant mass murderer to teach my children either. Nor, for that matter, an avowed Muslim, Buddhist, or atheist. Why? Is it because I hate these people? No! Absolutely not! It is a question of what lifestyles and virtues I want upheld for my children to value and emulate! In making these value judgments about the lifestyles and virtues I want promoted in front of my children, I am called, as a

Christian parent, to "be discriminating". I am not called to hate. No. But I am called to discriminate.

> *...whatever things are true, whatever things are noble, whatever things are just, whatever things are pure, whatever things are lovely, whatever things are of good report, if there is any virtue and if there is anything praiseworthy--meditate on these things.* (Phil 4:8)

Now, you may not necessarily agree with my personal stance on barring homosexuals from teaching my children. You may feel that I might be taking it too far. After all what teacher is perfect? Well not to put too fine a point on it, but I'm not talking about moral perfection. I'm talking about role models. There is a difference. It certainly is your right to think that my position is too absolute. But do you disagree that it is my right, both as a parent and as a Christian, to make this choice? In making this choice do you really think I'm advocating hatred? The only reason I ask is because I know that some Christians feel very uneasy about taking such a strong position on homosexuality. I don't think we need to feel uneasy about it. All I'm saying is that we need to establish boundaries, and in doing so we will necessarily make judgment calls.

I believe there are some things that are non-negotiable. I don't think that the state, or anyone else for that matter, has the right to make these decisions for me or for my children simply because they think it is okay for homosexuals to teach children. Again, virtue, not moral perfection, is fundamental to being a good role model and a good teacher. Virtues like chastity, sexual purity, honesty and loyalty to God are essential aspects of a proper education. The virtues that we as Christians are called to meditate upon above, (and presumably the virtues we are to teach our children as commanded in Deut. 6:6-90 and Deut. 11: 18-21) cannot be arrived at without exercising discrimination and discernment. But they can be arrived at without hatred.

To get back to the influences on my children, you should know that I am married to a teacher. I know first-hand that teachers pass on much more than simple facts. They influence the way children look at the world around them. I do not condone homosexuality. Therefore, I don't want a homosexual influencing my children. But what teacher is perfect, you ask? Again, I'm not talking about moral perfection. We all fall short of the glory of God. I am simply talking about the lifestyle that a teacher advocates. There is a big difference between a repentant and reformed sinner and a person who continues to advocate the breaking of the seventh commandment by the way they choose to live. A teacher who advocates pre-marital sex, marital infidelity, or homosexual behavior is not a candidate to teach my children. That is one of the reasons my children are not in the public school system.

It's not because the system is devoid of good teachers. In fact, the public system has some excellent teachers. But in that public system, I have no say in who teaches my children, and no say on what lifestyles, virtues, morals, and worldviews are presented for my children to emulate.

Perhaps you don't think I'm being nice, or fair. Well, when it comes to the education of my children being nice and fair has nothing to do with it. I love my children and protecting them while they are young and impressionable is a loving act. In fact it is fundamental to being a loving parent. So yes, I think Christian parents—in fact, parents in general—ought to be discriminating.

But having said this, you should also know that I don't condone calling homosexuals names, or being deliberately ignorant. Then again, is name calling the moral equivalent of a hate crime? Is this what the politician was suggesting at that meeting when he said, "not one act of discrimination should be tolerated"? Is this what Bill C-250 was all about? This is certainly the where Senator Serge Joyal (quoted at the start of this chapter) is going.

The Real Reason Behind Hate Crime Legislation

He believes that name-calling is equivalent to hate propaganda. If so, then homosexuals are fast becoming a privileged class of people. Because, let's be honest. Christians are subject to more pejorative name calling in North American society than any other group, and there's certainly no law being contemplated to protect us.

The thing that I've discovered in this whole sordid affair is that liberals and politically correct people love to hide behind purposefully ambiguous language. Bill C-250 was supposedly written to deal with hate crime. The logical mind would connect this to criminal acts like murder, theft and vandalism carried out with extreme contempt for the victims because of their "identifiable trait." But it appears that the bill's supporters want to stop name-calling and anything else that "hurts people's feelings." Think of all the words that don't sound nice. Words like "sodomy." Or "sodomite." Or "abomination." Or "shameful." Or "unnatural." Or "perversion." Or, God forbid, the word "sin."

Are these discriminatory words? Yes they are. They make judgment calls about certain people, practices, and lifestyles. But should uttering these words be considered equivalent to a hate crime? As a Christian, I certainly hope you don't think so. It is one thing to say that Christians should not use ignorant and inflammatory language when speaking to or about homosexuals. But that is entirely different from saying we shouldn't refer to homosexuals the way the Bible does.

Holding God's word to a politically correct standard is outrageous. Crass worldly terms like "faggot" or "queer" are certainly inappropriate. But Biblical words like "abomination," or "sodomite," are very appropriate. And here is why. The Bible's language is both judicious, meaning that *because* the Bible represents God's perspective it is not unjustly inflammatory but merely reflects His holy disposition, and it is inspired, meaning that the human authors under the superintendence of the Holy Spirit used the precise words that God had intended them to use. Therefore to argue that Christians shouldn't use this type of language is ultimately an attack on the doctrine of inspiration. The Bible is inspired from beginning to end. The whole of it. *And every single word of it.* As Jesus implied, every "jot and tittle" is judicious, including those harsh passages, precisely because the Bible is God's word on the matter, and it shall never pass away. (Matt. 5:18) But it too will be viewed as hate propaganda if the activists have their way.

Are Homosexuals Victims?

This leads me to the second reason why Bill C-250, and most other attempts to expand the definition of "hate crime" are untenable. The ambiguous language used to justify Bill C-250, which lumped discrimination in with hate crime, perpetuates the false notion that homosexuals are consistently victimized throughout Canada and the USA. Supporters argued that changing the Criminal Code to explicitly include "sexual orientation" would enable homosexuals to find legal remedy from the atrocities they suffer through hate-speech.

A little contextual history is in order here. The list of "identifiable groups" in the *Criminal Code* identifies groups that have suffered severe hate crimes on a large-scale in the relatively recent past. Legal scholars have pointed out that the term "identifiable group" is used only, and we must emphasize "*only,*" for groups of people who have innate and unchangeable characteristics (excepting religion of course which can be chosen), and who have suffered severe persecution, the kind of persecution that is genocidal.

Race and ethnicity were included under the hate crime's provision of the Code because these categories deal with innate characteristics—skin color, physical features—for which the group in question suffered atrocities. For example, in the West, black people and other people of color suffered atrocities on a large scale simply *because* of the color of their skin, the shape of the eyes, etc. Witness the history of slavery in North America. It was genocidal servitude based exclusively on race. This is why "race and ethnicity" were included as categories requiring protection. It was the history, the actual experience, that created the need to include "race and ethnicity" in the hate crime portion of the Code. The category of "religion," which is not an innate unchangeable characteristic, was added later to recognize the atrocities committed against Jews, who were persecuted in Nazi Germany.

In both cases, these identifiable groups, "race and ethnicity" and "religion", were included under the hate crime portion of the *Criminal Code of Canada* due to the history of severe, widespread, and consistent persecution. This was persecution that resulted in genocide, either by forced labor or systematic extermination. That is the point. People of color, whether black slaves in the United States, or Asians building the Canadian railroad, did suffer tremendously for no definable moral reason. So did those of an identifiable "religion", Judaism, during the Second World War. The nature and extent of the persecution of people identified in the Criminal Code is rooted in verifiable history.

Now, do homosexuals experience this kind of persecution today? The kind of persecution that is rooted in verifiable fact or history? No they do not. This begs the question: why would we include them in this section of the law? Of course, the homosexual activist may ask the same thing. "Do Blacks and Jews (still) experience this kind of persecution?" To ask the question is, in some sense, to answer it. We've come a long way in race relations. Blacks and Jews do not experience the same level of persecution that they once did, at least not here in North America. Homosexual activists may then ask that if this is indeed the case, why is there still a law to protect them. "If Blacks and Jews aren't experiencing massive persecution, why then do we need these laws at all?" This is, in some sense, a fair question.

In fact, let's explore it a little further. If Blacks and Jews no longer experience massive persecution, yet our law still provides protection for them, then why not apply the same standard to homosexuals? The homosexual activist will claim that, like Blacks and Jews, homosexuals experienced great persecution in the past. The activist will claim that the history of the Christian West is a history of genocide against homosexuals, and he will add that the Church is the primary instigator of this historic hatred. Homosexuals were denied basic rights. They were flogged, beaten, punished, sanctioned and "exterminated" by the state, all in the name of Christian morality. So even though homosexuals are not experiencing persecution today, they did in the past. Hate crime law, they would argue, would ensure that the past would never be repeated; that there will never be a sexual "inquisition" again.

The complaint that homosexuals have suffered injustice under the dominance of Christianity may resonate with some Christians today. They must keep in mind, however, the historic differences. Christian civilizations in the past millennia viewed homosexual acts as social deviant behavior (a view endorsed by the Criminal Code of Canada until Pierre Trudeau change the laws forbidding sodomy in 1969). As a result, sodomy was a criminal act. The state believed that sodomy left unchecked would specifically harm and pervert the family, and generally corrupt society. Therefore, the state suppressed the behavior because such was its mandate by God (to defend the noble and God-ordained institutions of society: family and church etc.,). The homosexual activist would have us believe that the state had no moral authority to suppress the behavior and therefore concludes wrongly that homosexuals suffered unjustly under Christian states. But this ignores the theological and moral underpinnings of historic Christian jurisprudence. The fact that sexual attitudes and the law regarding these activities have changed does not mean that homosexuals suffered unjustly in the past. Would they argue that murders, rapists, thieves, adulterers, and those guilty of incest suffered "persecution" under a Christian regime as well, and continue to under secular governments (excepting of course, adultery—which apparently now is acceptable behavior)?

Granted, attitudes have changed. Many Christians no longer accept the traditional social view of sodomy. Trudeau's statement, the "state has no business in the bedrooms of the nation," has had a profound effect on the moral and social philosophy of most Christians today. Christians certainly don't condone witch-hunts, entrapment, incivility or an inquisition directed at homosexuals. But this is all beside the point. Homosexuals may choose to draw a parallel between themselves and the treatment of Blacks and Jews but there is a fundamental difference that distinguishes their histories. There is absolutely no moral equivalence between Blacks, Jews, and Asians on the one hand, and homosexuals on the other. Blacks, Asians, and Jews are what they are by birth, not by their behavior or actions. Race is an immutable, or unchangeable, characteristic. (I realize that some people convert to Judaism as a faith, but I'm speaking here of Jews as an ethnic group.) Homosexuality is not an immutable characteristic. Homosexuals are not "born that way."

Race and ethnicity are not a matter of choice, either biologically or morally. Sexual preference is. I realize that homosexuals want to debate this point, *but that is the point.* From the religious, theological standpoint the evidence is conclusive—homosexuality is not innate. God did not create anyone "gay." Homosexuality is a learned and chosen lifestyle. There may be extenuating circumstances that influence a person's choice. These influences may even be unknown on a conscious level. Early childhood development deeply influences everyone. Traumatic experiences such as the lack of a loving father, or sexual child abuse, can deeply affect the subconscious. However, these traumatic childhood experiences do not override the force of the human will. In the final analysis it is the human will which is the source of our sexual orientation and therefore same sex attraction is ultimately chosen.

The Bible teaches us that the source of man's *orientation*, his desires and his actions is the human heart—in other words the human will.

- *Keep your heart with all diligence, For out of it spring the issues of life.* (Prov. 4:23)

- *The heart is deceitful above all things, and desperately wicked; who can know it? I, the LORD, search the heart, I test the mind...* (Jer 17:9-10)

- *Therefore God also gave them up to uncleanness, in the lusts of their hearts, to dishonor their bodies among themselves...* (Rom. 1:24)

Does the environment influence? Yes it does. But the environment does not replace or eliminate the place of man's will to be who he is. It is because we choose to follow our heart's desire that God holds us responsible for our actions, desires and our orientation.

You might ask "Yeah, but what about all those Christians who say otherwise?" To which I would respond, "Yeah, and what about Judas -- wasn't he a disciple of Christ too?" Some people claim to be Christian, yet hold spurious views about what the Bible teaches. The fact is that those who claim homosexuality is an "innate characteristic" are way out on a theological *and scientific* limb. Their interpretations of the Bible are so out of step with universal Christian tradition and confessions that it's absolutely laughable to me that the secular media (which always goes out of its way to ridicule Christianity) considers their position "authoritative". The very idea of explaining away the sin of homosexuality, which is explicitly how it is described in the Bible, denies the power of Christ to forgive and change sinners, including homosexuals.

Furthermore, the scientific data on the "innateness" of homosexuality is completely flawed.

The Real Reason Behind Hate Crime Legislation

Even one of the psychiatrists who led the charge in 1973 for the American Psychiatric Association to remove homosexuality from its diagnostic manual of "recognized mental disorders", is now having second thoughts. Dr. Robert Spitzer is Chief of Biometrics Research and Professor of Psychiatry at Columbia University in New York City. See here how he has changed his mind:

> *Like most psychiatrists, I thought that homosexual behavior could only be **resisted**, and that no one could really change their sexual orientation. I now believe that to be false. Some people **can** and **do** change. Contrary to conventional wisdom, some highly motivated individuals, using a variety of change efforts, can make substantial change in multiple indicators of sexual orientation.* (Emphasis in the original)[6]

Dr. Spitzer's findings involved 200 men and women who have experienced a "significant shift from homosexual to heterosexual attraction, and have sustained this shift for at least five years." The study also found that 67% of the men who had rarely or never felt any opposite-sex attraction before the change effort now report "significant heterosexual attraction." [7]

If there is a scientific basis for believing homosexuals are born and not made, it has not come to light. The science is inconclusive, and laws should never be based on inconclusive science. A law, to be a just law, *cannot* be based upon pending scientific evidence. To date, all the rhetoric surrounding gay marriage and hate crime law is based in part on the unproven supposition that homosexuals are born "gay" just like Blacks and Jews are born that way. This is absolute propaganda and it is time for Christians to say so.

Statistics On Hate Crime

Of course, not every homosexual relies on the scientific "we-were-born-this-way" argument. "In a just society", they will claim, "a hate crime should be prosecuted regardless of whether a homosexual is born 'gay' or has chosen his 'orientation'." Their argument is that homosexuals continue to experience discrimination and hate crime today precisely because of their homosexuality. And that, they say, is why laws like Bill C-250 are necessary. Well, let's look at the statistic on "hate crime" toward homosexuals.

Let's start with the fundamental question. Based on the *facts*, is there reason to believe that homosexuals suffer disproportionately more hate and violence than any other group in society? Are we supposed to believe that at present in Canada, or in North America for that matter, homosexuals are experiencing a level of discrimination that necessitates a change to any law or criminal code?

Let's look at some American statistics first. The FBI Uniform Crime Reporting Program (UCR) established that in 2001, there were 9,730 "bias-motivated incidents" across the continental United States. That's not 9,730 hate crimes against homosexuals; that's the total of all hate crime under every category for that year.

Let's put it into perspective. In 2001 when this report was filed, "nearly 17,000" law enforcement agencies nationwide participated in the Uniform Crime Reporting Program. That includes almost all policing agencies in the United States. Collectively these agencies represent almost 242 million people in America, about 85% of the country's population.

Out of the 9,730 hate crimes reported, 4,367 (44.9%) were race related, 2,098 (21.6%) were ethnically based, 1,828 (18.8%) were related to religion, and only 1,393 (14.3%) were based on sexual orientation. Additionally, there were 35 (0.4%) incidents of hate crime against the disabled.

In analyzing the data on homosexual hate crime, some other interesting information is revealed. Of those 1,393 sexual orientation hate crimes, 930 were anti-male homosexual, 205 anti-female homosexual, 173 anti-homosexual, 17 anti-bisexual and 18 anti-heterosexual in nature. The combined gay, lesbian, and bisexual total of hate crime comes to 1,325 incidents. That means out of a population base of 241.8 *million* people, a total of just over 1300—a truly miniscule percentage—were victims of homosexual hate crime. This is hardly on the same level or scale as the Jewish Holocaust or black slavery.

But that's the United States. What about Canada? In Canada's largest city, Toronto, the Toronto Police Department Hate Crimes Report for 2001 was proportionally similar to the U.S. experience. In 2001 in a city of 2 million people, there were 338 hate crime incidents reported. Of that total, 24 were homosexual hate crimes. In their 2002 report the number dropped to 11. The report also tracked the number of homosexual hate crimes since 1993; 211 incidents over the span of 10 years in a city of 2million does not constitute a major crisis in hate crime perpetrated against homosexuals.

The arguments that were used to support Bill C-250 were hysterical. Rather than raise genuine awareness of indignities that homosexuals may experience, Bill C-250 trivialized the very real suffering of Blacks and Jews who *did* endure unbearable conditions. The scale and consistency of their persecutions far exceeded *anything* that homosexuals may have experienced. Remember once again, that homosexuality is not the moral equivalent of race or ethnicity. It is not an inherent trait. It is a chosen "orientation".

Are we really to believe that homosexuals suffer so badly that a categorical change to the *Criminal Code of Canada* is necessary? Or, for that matter, a change to the U.S. Constitution? Is discrimination against homosexuals happening? I have already conceded that it is. But is there any more discrimination against homosexuals than there is against any other "identifiable group" in Canada? No. Certainly no more than the ridicule that is heaped on sincere, Bible-believing Christians in newspapers across our "tolerant" continent.

But more importantly, if homosexuals are so severely discriminated against, how is it that so many of them enjoy very highly paid and high profile positions in society? Homosexuals rank among some of the most affluent and influential citizens of our two countries. (Look at Hollywood. Look at governments. Look at the music industry.) Which truly begs the question: where is all this discrimination? Where is the *evidence* that homosexuals suffer hate crime on the same level that Jews and blacks did? Or the way thousands of Christians do today in many places around the world?

The very notion that there is a need for hate crime law to protect homosexuals is propaganda. I realize that what I'm saying isn't politically correct. I also fully expect that someone, somewhere, will try to have me charged (perhaps under the type of law I am criticizing in this book), with a hate crime for denying that homosexuals suffer on a genocidal level. Or for trivializing the discrimination they face every day simply because of their "orientation." I realize there are some who would accuse me of advocating sexual genocide for insisting that homosexuality is not innate, but chosen. Frankly, that is a risk I am prepared to take for speaking the truth.

Fred Phelps Is An Aberration

For some time in Canada, the movement to criminalize moral objection to homosexuality has been gathering steam. Activists have used Fred Phelps as an example of the stereotypical Christian approach. This is just foolish. Fred Phelps is the man who used to run a website called "godhatesfaggots.com". A man who the media says supported the murder of a young homosexual in the American Midwest.

It amazes me that we Christians actually take it seriously when our detractors try to paint us all with the "Fred Phelps brush". Just imagine if we were to go on a cross-country tour decrying the hate-speech of "artists" like Marilyn Manson and holding all liberals accountable for his work.

Maybe you've never heard of Marilyn Manson. He (yes, "Marilyn" is a guy) is a "goth-rock" artist who is famous for statements like: *"Hopefully, I'll be remembered as the person who brought an end to Christianity."* ("Spin" Magazine, August 1996, p. 34). He has said many nasty things about Christianity. Here's a particular choice quote from his website (please note the language is very graphic. I've edited out the words that would offend, without destroying the thrust of what is being said. It wasn't easy):

> *Invest in YOU, and put the bible-belt-wearing- pro life-red-neck-record-burning- fundamentalist- f*g-bashing hypocrites out of business so they can wallow in their own self-made, feeble-minded Hell. Hallelujah mother******s!*

> *There's a hurricane a-blowing, and just by knowing what you know, you have an advantage over the blind morons that surround you every day. However, not everyone can be saved. Civilize those you can and @*&! the rest. There are too many people in this world. It is not our responsibility to be constantly cleaning up after the weak-minded. Nature will eventually run its course, and those too senseless to survive will fortunately be crushed beneath the wheels of our progress.*

> *America should be very, very afraid. They have found it hard to accept the monster that they have created. The stupid ones who doubt me/you will surely be destroyed. I am the all-American AntiChrist. I have predicted the past; I am the accuser.*

So the next time some politically correct proponent of hate crime legislation throws Fred Phelps in your face, just remind him that for every Fred, there are at least 100 Marilyns, all with a lot more money and influence to pervert the minds of the young masses.

5 | Hate Crime Data: A Detailed Analysis

The success of the Program rests with the law enforcement officers who determine that a bias motivation does indeed exist. **FBI Uniform Crime Report**

L et's look a little further at the statistics on hate crime. We have already established that there really is no "epidemic" of violence against homosexuals. But it's enlightening to understand where the epidemic idea originates. After all, *someone* convinced Canada's parliamentarians that there was and is a problem. But the argument was based not just on deceptive statistics, but also on faulty science.

Bill C-250 was based, in part, on the argument that police agencies have uncovered evidence that hate crime against homosexuals is a problem. As we've already seen, the statistics don't support that. Simply put, it's a lie. But there is more to the story. Not only is there not a serious hate crime epidemic against homosexuals, the statistical data that establishes *any hate crime at all* against homosexuals is highly suspect. This questionable data is another reason to question the need for Bill C-250 or its equivalent.

There are four fundamental flaws in the "science" of hate crime investigation:

1) police agencies are politically motivated,
2) hate crime investigation is subjective,
3) many investigators rely on the victim's perception of the crime and,
4) gay-on-gay crime is not considered in hate crime analysis.

These four flaws seriously compromise the statistical data on hate crime, and in turn, cast doubt on the need for legal protection of homosexuals.

Police Agencies Are Politically Motivated

Police investigation is an objective science. At least it is supposed to be. Democratic societies have a vested interest in the clinical, objective posture of their police departments. If outside political pressure or internal bureaucracy and politics are not stemmed, the reputation of police officers will decline. Police departments are sensitive for the most part to such a charge, which is why police investigation is viewed as a science. It is necessary that objective scientific standards be maintained. Police agencies wield significant power in our society. But if the science of investigation can be manipulated, if the procedures by which investigations in the field, in the forensic lab and finally at the statistical level can be "massaged" to conform to a political ideology, the judicial system as a whole will be shaken. People will simply lose their confidence in those entrusted to keep law and order. It is precisely on this point, on the concept of policing done as an objective science, that hate crime investigations are failing the confidence test.

The FBI's Uniform Crime Reporting Program (UCR), indicated in 2001 that clinical objectivity is not its main concern. Of course, it didn't quite put it that way. But the point was made nevertheless:

The Real Reason Behind Hate Crime Legislation

*Law enforcement investigation is critical to the determination process because it must reveal sufficient evidence as to whether the offender's actions were motivated, in whole or in part, by bias. **For this reason, the success of the Program rests with the law enforcement officers who determine that a bias motivation does indeed exist.*** [Emphasis added]

As it stands, there is nothing wrong with a bureaucracy's desire to see a specific program succeed. The problem in this case however lies with the UCR's definition of success. In the report, the UCR states that the "success of the Program" rests on finding "bias" or "hate" in a crime. This admission indicates that, at least on one level, objectivity has been compromised. From a genuinely objective standpoint, success would be defined by the department's ability to distinguish between "regular" crime and "hate" crime. In other words, the program's goal should be to identify objectively if a crime is hate motivated. The goal should be trying to determine if "hate crime" exists. But as the report indicates, the program will be considered successful if investigators find that "biases" exist. Read that line again.

For this reason, the success of the Program rests with the law enforcement officers who determine that a bias motivation does indeed exist.

Admittedly this is a subtle point and it may not seem all that important. But the fact that the UCR report does not clarify its own commitment to objective investigative procedure does little to assure the public that hate crime investigation is not driven by arbitrary ideologies. This is a potentially significant flaw in the way hate crime statistics would be generated. At the very least, it is a compromise of the investigative science, and it leads very easily to a suspicion that claims of hate crime against the homosexual community are prone to exaggeration.

Hate Crime Investigation Is Subjective

If the above invites suspicion, this second flaw should truly raise red flags. Police departments readily admit that hate crime analysis is largely a subjective science. To understand the serious nature of such an admission, a definition of hate crime is in order. The UCR report defines it as follows:

> *Hate crimes are not separate, distinct crimes; instead, they are traditional offences motivated by the offender's bias . . . rather than create new crime categories, program developers felt that collecting additional information about crimes already being reported to the UCR Program would fulfil the directives addressed in the Hate Crime Statistic Act.*

It is important to note that the report acknowledged that there is no difference between a "regular" crime, and a "hate" crime in terms of the act committed. A hate crime is not a different type of crime. It has the same variables. In fact, hate crime is categorized in the same way as regular crime: crimes against persons (murder and non-negligent manslaughter, forcible rape, aggravated assault, simple assault, and intimidation), *crimes against property* (robbery, burglary, larceny-theft, motor vehicle theft, arson, and destruction/damage/vandalism of property), and *crimes against society* (any combination of the above directed at individuals or a group).

So what distinguishes a hate crime from regular, run-of-the-mill lawbreaking? The only difference is motive. "Hate crimes are not separate, distinct crimes; instead, they are traditional offences motivated by the offender's bias."

This is the second major flaw with all statistical hate crime data related to homosexuality. Anyone will tell you that discovering the "motive" of an offender in any crime is an elusive science. In most cases it involves the subjective input of the investigator who interprets the evidence in accord with what "probably" motivated the offender. The problem is, the offender isn't usually around to tell the investigator, is most often unknown to the victim, and very often never apprehended. The investigator is left to make a judgement call. Hate crime investigation is not an exact science. The UCR report states it this way:

> *Because motivation is subjective, it is difficult to know with certainty whether a crime was the result of the offender's bias. Law enforcement investigation is critical to the determination process because it must reveal sufficient evidence as to whether the offender's actions were motivated, in whole or in part, by bias.*

So again, it is not an exact science. But police agencies are willing to tackle the complex issues of human motive, even without questioning the offender. It doesn't take a rocket scientist to understand that within these imperfect investigative parameters, the pressure (both internal and external) to come up with the "existence of bias" will drive some investigators to stretch their conclusions.

The Victim Decides

The principles of hate crime investigation are so subjective that police agencies are admitting they rely on the "perception" of the victim in determining the existence of hate crime. Ironically, police agencies recognize the conflict this policy presents and thus offer a type of disclaimer. The UCR report stated the following:

> *Law enforcement reports an incident as a hate crime **only if the investigation revealed sufficient, objective facts** to lead a reasonable and prudent person to conclude that the offender's actions were motivated, in whole or in part, by bias against a racial, religious . . . or sexual-orientation group.* [Emphasis added]

This sounds good until you dig deeper to find out what those "sufficient, objective facts" are. You discover there are none. This reinforces the serious problems that are inherent in conducting an investigation based largely on subjective feelings rather than fact. But all is not lost. The Toronto Police Department, which operates on the same premise and system as the FBI hate crime unit, offers the following description of what is sufficient in its 2001 hate crime report.

> *Comments and/or actions of a suspect during an incident are significant in helping to determine the suspect's motive and bias; however, it is sometimes difficult to classify an occurrence. Other criteria used to assist in classifying occurrences include the **victim's** perception of the incident, motives, significant dates, symbols and history of the community.* [Emphasis added]

In other words, because offenders are rarely available, the investigators rely on the victim's assessment. Let's put this into a real life situation. A young man holds up another man in an alley. The man squeals in fear. The attacker, unaware at first that his victim is gay, knocks the man down, steals his wallet, and then, learning or guessing the sexual orientation/proclivity of his victim, screams, "You ...."

The offender's criminal intent was robbery. The fact that his victim was a homosexual had nothing to do with his motive. In fact, it was completely incidental to the crime. The mugger might have contempt for his victim's homosexuality, but that had nothing to do with the motive for the crime. The motive was money. He had a drug habit and needed cash in a hurry. The homosexual happened to be in the wrong place at the wrong time. But consider the investigation. As it becomes apparent that the assailant won't be apprehended, investigators must rely on the victim's assessment. How do you think the victim, in this case the homosexual, will perceive what has happened to him? This hypothetical situation would, under the Toronto

Police Department's definition above, almost certainly be recorded in the statistical annals as a "hate crime".

This scenario is not unique. It happens more often than is acknowledged in official police records. The point is that because hate crime investigation relies on the perception of the victim, the statistical data on homosexual hate crime is vulnerable to corruption by facts, perceptions, and circumstances that are anything but purely scientific.

Is Gay-on-Gay Violence A Hate Crime?

The final factor that affects the reliability of the statistics on hate crime against homosexuals is the incidence of gay-on-gay crime. In the present political climate, very few people will acknowledge that this long-standing and growing problem exists. Right now, if a gay man is killed in the dead of night in a public park of a major city, it is generally assumed that a skinhead gay-basher was responsible. When gay men are intimidated as they're coming out of a bar, it is assumed that skinheads are responsible. Why? Because most people think in stereotypes. Everyone knows that gay men don't shave their heads. They don't wear black leather. And they certainly don't beat on the men they "love", right?

Nothing exposes the ideological blindness of hate crime law proponents more than this issue. Gay-on-gay crime is happening all across this country, yet few acknowledge it. Island and Letellier, the authors of <u>Men Who Beat The Men Who Love Them</u>, (already cited in an earlier context), estimate that half a million gay men in America are abused by their lovers every year. For example, they write:

> *The Gay Men's Domestic Violence Project at the Community United Against Violence (CUAV) in San Francisco estimates that for every police incident report on gay men's domestic violence that CUAV receives, there are between 10 and 20 incidents that go unreported.*

Clearly, not only are gay men victims of domestic violence, but they are being battered at an alarming rate.

The problem with gay-on-gay crime is that it is viewed as a lovers' spat.

The 'boys being boys' idea may have been harmless when we were all six years old, but when a man is 26 years old, is in the hospital with broken bones, and his lover broke them, this is not normal! This is much more than boys being boys. It is violence. Unfortunately, this myth is pervasive in the gay male community. With few positive relationship role models available, many gay men tend to view and accept violence by their partners as the norm.

Viewing this behavior as normative for gay relationships is not unusual. The homosexual community accepts it as part of their maleness. Neither is it abnormal for the heterosexual community to expect homosexuals to be violent. Island and Letellier point out that until recently the San Francisco Police Department refused to recognize criminal violence that was taking place in homosexual relationships.

The police have been unwilling to even acknowledge gay male relationships, and their inability or unwillingness to see men as victims has influenced their underreporting of gay men's domestic violence. Until just recently, most cases of gay domestic violence have been reported as "mutual combat" ...

Clearly, under-reporting is not the same as reporting gay-on-gay crime as a type of hate crime. So what does all this have to do with hate crime legislation? Again, it centers on the assumptions that police departments and investigators make. The trouble with hate crime is that in most cases it is anonymous. The offender is usually unknown to the victim. Most police agencies assume when a gay man is beaten, assaulted, or otherwise injured, (and the offender is not apprehended), that the crime was perpetrated by a straight male who has a strong bias against gay men. Yet, there is a lot of evidence that gay men are also inflicting this kind of violence *on one another*. Violence is a fundamental aspect of the gay culture, whether this is acknowledged or not. In fact, a higher proportion of violence takes place in the homosexual community. Is it therefore beyond the realm of possibility that a homosexual would anonymously beat on other gay men, "just because"? Would it be impossible that gay men could beat, harass and intimidate other gay men, and make it look like a "gay-basher" hate crime?

Political Agendas Are The Real Hate Crime

The reality is that political agendas are driving our policing agencies. The very idea that police departments approach hate crime objectively in today's climate is a farce. The concept of hate crime is grounded on an imperfect science. It involves the input of the victim, even when the victim does not know his assailant. It refuses to take into account the reality of violence and the propensity for crime within the gay community itself.

When proponents of Bill C-250 speak of hate crime versus regular crime, what they are really talking about is politically incorrect crime versus politically acceptable crime. In other words, if a black man breaks into a rich white man's home and murders the owner, rapes the man's wife and steals the valuables out of the house, what we have is a crime. But it's a "plain old crime", not a "hate crime", because it doesn't fit the hate crime criteria. The crime may have been motivated by envy, but class envy is politically acceptable today. But let some punk call a homosexual a nasty name and punch his lights out, and we have a hate crime.

Of course on one level, all of this could be considered amusing. Or at least absurd. Ask yourself this. If there is such a thing as "hate crime", does that mean there is also something called "non-hateful crime"? "Benevolent crime", maybe? But seriously, since when has bias *not* been a governing factor in any crime? When Cain murdered his brother Abel, was bias not involved? Or did it happen on a whim? What about hate? Did Cain hate his brother, or did he murder him without malice aforethought? As he was beating the life out of Abel, was he saying, "don't take this personal bro... this is just something I gotta do...."? All of this would be funny if it wasn't so politically pathetic.

6

Undefined Terms Make Bad Law

Rights. RIGHTS! RIGHTS? For sexual deviant . . . sexual behavior there are now rights. That's what I'm worried about with the pedophilia and the bestiality and the sadomasochism and the cross-dressing. Is this all going to be 'rights' too, to deviant sexual behavior? It's deviant sexual behavior. Why does deviant sexual behavior get rights? I don't understand that to start out with.— **Dr. Laura Schlesinger**

There is another problem with Bill C-250 as it was drafted, and indeed with virtually all hate crime laws. It is always bad law in terms of its legal text. The very notion of protecting something or someone requires that we know precisely what quality, trait, or specific action it is that is being protected. Clearly, terms that are not properly defined in law make for very bad law. And protection based on sexual orientation is fuzzy, unclear and undefined. In most hate crime laws, including Bill C-250 as it almost passed through both houses of the Canadian Parliament, the operative term was not "homosexual." It was "sexual orientation." As a legal term, "sexual orientation" was not defined. It is precisely because of this imprecision in the definition that the law was so dangerous. Bill C-250, as it was written, would have left a huge amount of latitude for judicial interpretation; judges would decide exactly what the term might or might not mean.

Now you might be thinking that I'm just saying this to provoke a reaction. Or as one Member of Parliament loudly screamed at me, (and my dear friend Royal Hamel, who was the main object of this MP's tirade) at a town hall meeting in Waterloo, Ontario: "You're a bigot! A bigot! A hate monger!" All because in a sidebar discussion I had with the MP, I had affirmed the precise point above. Or, perhaps, you may even be thinking that I'm fear mongering. I assure you that I am not, nor am I any of the names the MP called Reverend Hamel or myself.

Despite what this MP thinks, it is clear from homosexual literature that "sexual orientation" includes not only adult same-sex inclination and activity (male and female homosexuality), but also bisexual interests and transgenderism. However, this hardly exhausts the lists of alternative "sexual orientations."

As an example of how broadly the term can be applied, medical and academic experts have argued that exhibitionism, fetishism, transvestism, voyeurism, sadomasochism and pedophilia should be removed from the *Diagnostic and Statistical Manual of Mental Disorders*. As recently as six years ago, the *American Psychological Association* determined that pedophilia, which they euphemistically referred to as "intergenerational sex," may not be harmful and therefore considered removing pedophilia from the list of disorders.[8]

The correlation between homosexuality and pederasty (sex between a man and a boy) is far more prevalent than the mainstream media is willing to report. In fact, many homosexual activist organizations are not only willing to acknowledge the connection; they are actively promoting it under the guise of "sexual freedom" for children.

The Real Reason Behind Hate Crime Legislation

In 1972, the *National Coalition of Gay Organizations* in the United States included in its list of gay rights, the "repeal of all laws governing the age of sexual consent." [9] Their demands have not changed. Homosexual activists are aggressively challenging traditional standards of human sexuality, by insisting that "child sexual liberation" is a fundamental outworking of gay and human rights.

To camouflage the natural vileness and abuse such "child sexual liberation" entails, and to gain the approval of the so-called "straight" mainstream of society, homosexual activists have changed the focus of the debate. Instead of speaking about promiscuous sex or sexual license, they speak about human rights. Furthermore, instead of speaking about child molestation they use academically acceptable euphemisms like, "intergenerational sex," "intergenerational intimacy," "male generational intimacy." Moreover, pedophiles are no longer referred to as child molesters, but just another persecuted "sexual minority." Those who oppose this form of "love" are branded as "sexual ageists" and "child-sex-oppressors". [10] An editorial in the July 1995 homosexual magazine *Guide*, said that:

> *Kids are still being taught destructive lies about sex. They are told that until they are 16 (or 14 or some other arbitrary age that varies from state to state) . . . any sexual expression on their part means a crime is being committed. We can be proud that the gay movement has been home to the few voices who have had the courage to say out loud that children are naturally sexual, that they deserve the right to sexual expression with whoever they choose . . . Instead of being labeled pedophiles, we must proudly proclaim that sex is good, including children's sexuality. Surrounded by pious moralists with deadening anti-sexual rules, we must be shameless rule-breakers, demonstrating our allegiance to a higher concept (of) love. We must do it for the children's sake.*

The correlation between pedophilia and homosexuality is so strong that Zackie Achmat from South Africa's *(AIDS) Treatment Action Campaign* describes his first sexual experience in the book *Defiant Desire* as, "My Childhood as an Adult Molester."[11]   At ten years of age, an adult man in a public washroom sexually molested him. He refers to this experience as a positive event which gave him the confidence to actualize his deep sexual drive, a drive that compelled him, he said, to go back to the public washrooms to be repeatedly sodomized by two to three men daily. As he says, if anyone was guilty of a sexual crime, he was guilty of "adult molestation."

Kevin Bishop, a homosexual and an admitted pedophile, is very frank about the relationship between homosexuality and child molestation: "Scratch the average homosexual," he writes, "and you will find a pedophile." Bishop promotes the work of NAMBLA, the North American Man/Boy Love Association. He is on a crusade to abolish laws governing the age of sexual consent in his home country of South Africa. He believes that children must be sexually empowered. We must, he writes, "(teach) them about loving relationships at an early age, and give them the opportunity to make an informed decision about having sex." In concert with these efforts, the international Rene Guyon Society uses the slogan: "Sex before eight, or it's too late."

These disturbing trends in human sexuality necessitate that at the very least a phrase like "sexual orientation" must have proscribed limits in law. If it is not defined it will open the door to allow practitioners of every conceivable sexual disorder to claim protection from hate propaganda under laws like Bill C-250. The term "sexual orientation" is an elastic, transient term that is not defined.

7 Judicial Protection For Whom?

The restrictions against same-sex marriage is an offence to the dignity of lesbians and gays because it limits the range of relationship options available to them [and] conveys the ominous message that they are unworthy of marriage. **–Harry LaForme, Ontario Superior Court Justice**

My MP (that's the Canadian equivalent to a Congressman) sent me a form letter recently. He sent it out to everyone in his electoral district. He wasn't particularly happy with the Town Hall meeting I had organized at the beginning of the summer of 2003. He wanted to address the concerns of his Christian constituents who had become motivated to speak out on Bill C-250. As a member of the governing party, my MP supported the bill.

In the mail-out, he pointed out that "provisions relating to hate propaganda are very specific . . . hate propaganda means to willfully incite hatred." Then he made the following comment:

> *I don't think the intent of any Canadian who is opposed to homosexuality on moral grounds is*

advocating hatred; they are simply expressing their opinion, which is protected under the Charter of Rights and Freedoms.

Now this seems quite reassuring. It is comforting to know that at least my MP doesn't view moral criticism of homosexual behavior as a hate crime. I was beginning to think every member of Canada's Liberal Party had lost his or her mind.

But there is an obvious problem. My MP isn't a judge. And right now in Canada, judges rule the day. I wouldn't trust most Canadian judges to throw me a life preserver if I were drowning. Judicial activism is destroying this country, as it is in America. Judges act *as de facto* gods, and we, the people, have absolutely no recourse to deal with judicial activism.

If judges believe a law is outmoded, outdated, not in step with their interpretation of the spirit of our Charter of Rights and Freedoms, they simply order government to re-write the laws, or rule those laws "unconstitutional." This is precisely how "gay marriage" became legal in Canada.

A lower-level Ontario court with three justices on a panel ruled that the current marriage law, which defined marriage as a union between a man and a woman, was "unconstitutional," and ordered the province of Ontario to immediately issue marriage licenses to "gay" couples whom desired to wed. A similar court issued an almost identical ruling at the other end of the country in British Columbia. The federal government could have appealed the decisions to the Supreme Court of Canada but opted instead, with no public consultation, to rewrite the law to recognize the "fundamental rights" of homosexuals. With those two decisions, Canada was thrown into cultural and moral chaos and homosexuals (many, incidentally, from the United States), converged on Toronto and Vancouver to have their "marriages" solemnized, often with the overt blessing of "tolerant" clergy in the Unitarian, United and Anglican denominations.

The Real Reason Behind Hate Crime Legislation

But back to my MP and his mail-out. I'm sure this man would never accuse a Christian of a hate crime for actively promoting historic Christian teaching on human sexuality. But then again, he is not a judge, and therein lies the problem.

The Liberal Deception

There was a "protection clause" in Bill C-250 but it was a meaningless carrot the federal government dangled in front of religious groups. Even though the government never formally sponsored Bill C-250, it was the governing Liberals who kept it alive while it was being studied in committee. On the third and final reading of the bill, Justice Minister Martin Cauchon made it clear that his government would support the bill.

Moreover, my MP repeatedly reminded me that the government had proposed an amendment, an amendment his party obviously hoped would lull conservative Christians back to sleep. That amendment would have exempted people from prosecution under the Bill C-250 if they were arguing against homosexuality…

> … *in good faith, (and) expressed or attempted to establish by an argument an opinion on a religious subject or an opinion based on a belief in a religious text.*

It is difficult see how this substantially improved on the original, which exempted:

> *(O)pinion(s) or argument(s) on a religious subject (that were) expressed in good faith…*

The addition of "religious text" was the only major enhancement. But this really was all very irrelevant. It was a smoke screen to cover the obvious. Christians would have been no more protected than they were before.

Why? Because the law itself is not the ultimate problem. The problem is, and has been for some time, activist judges. No "protection clause" can protect us from them. In Alberta, for example, the legislature had explicitly decided that the province's Individual Rights Protection Act would not include the term "sexual orientation". But the Supreme Court of Canada, in the Delwin Vriend case, simply overruled the elected government and *rewrote that law.* The Court said the Act would henceforth and forevermore be *interpreted* to include protection for homosexuals even if the province didn't want it, and whether or not the legislators rewrote that change into the act. We are fooling ourselves if we think judges wouldn't do the same with hate crime laws even though the law is written to "protect" religious expression in the debate on homosexuality. This is the final reason why bills like C-250 are bad laws. They give activist judges the legal tools to wage war on Christian morality.

Judicial Activism In Canada

If you think the case for judicial activism is overstated, I want to cite some more of the Canadian rulings that have compromised freedom of religion in Canada. These rulings demonstrate that our judiciary and our human rights tribunals generally view homosexual rights as absolute, while religious rights for Christians are second-rate at best.

In 1997 the Ontario Human Rights Commission in London, Ontario found that the city's mayor, Diane Haskett, was in violation of the Human Rights Code because of her refusal to declare a Gay Pride Day.

The same year Hugh Owens of Saskatchewan was brought before the Human Rights Tribunal of Saskatchewan for placing an ad in the Saskatoon *Star Phoenix* to coincide with Gay Pride Week. I've already referred to this case in the Preface to this book. But there is more to the story. The tribunal ordered Hugh Owens to pay the complainants $1,500 for their ordeal. Mr.

The Real Reason Behind Hate Crime Legislation

Owens' ordeal, however, was not over. In December 2002, the Saskatchewan Court of Queen's Bench ruled that he had indeed been "promoting hate" in his newspaper ad. It is very important to note that this second ruling was from a **court**. Not a "human rights tribunal", but a court in Saskatchewan. The ruling has already set a precedent that the promotion of conservative religious ideology in a public forum constitutes hate propaganda. So much for my MP's assurances.

There are more cases. In 1998, Ray Brillinger, a member of the Canadian Gay and Lesbian Archives, brought a complaint against Toronto printer, Scott Brockie, because Mr. Brockie refused to print an order for the Gay and Lesbian Archives on grounds that the material violated his conscience. The Human Rights Commission ordered Mr. Brockie to pay a fine of $5,000 and to provide the printing services to the Gay and Lesbian Archives. In the initial ruling, the sole adjudicator found that there is never a time when business can be withheld on the grounds of moral conflict. However, the court later reversed its decision stating that Mr. Brockie could refuse to print material if he could "reasonably prove" that there was a direct conflict between printing the material and his religious convictions. The problem however, was that the court rejected the grounds for his "conflict" and ordered him to print the material all the same.

In 2001, Trinity Western University, a Christian university in British Columbia, was denied the right to establish a teacher's training course by the BC College of Teachers, because the university had a "discriminatory policy". Under the policy, the students had to sign a document promising to refrain from practices the Bible condemned, including premarital sex and homosexuality. This case went to the Supreme Court of Canada, which ruled that religious rights in the Charter of Rights and Freedoms must be balanced by equality rights. In the Court's opinion the balance is maintained by belief and conduct. A person may have the freedom to believe a religious opinion, but the freedom to practice that belief in public is not equal.

Finally, in 2002, Mark Hall, who was refused permission by the Catholic School Board of Oshawa, Ontario to bring his homosexual partner to the school prom, was granted an injunction against the school by an Ontario Superior Court. The court ruled that the school violated the student's right, and that the right of the individual superceded the right of a religious institution.

There are many other cases that could be mentioned, including the ongoing struggle of Chris Kempling, a B.C. teacher who had his teaching license suspended because he wrote a letter to the editor of his local newspaper expressing his opinion on homosexuality.

These rulings have placed severe limitations on the freedom of religion in Canada, and serve as a backdrop, a cultural context if you will, by which we can judge the "protection" clause of Bill C-250. If the Saskatchewan Court of Queen's Bench can rule that the promotion of historic Christianity on the matter of homosexuality is hate propaganda, and if the Ontario Superior Court can rule that an individual's rights supercede the rights of a religious institution, and if the Supreme Court of Canada has determined that the "freedom of belief is not equal to the freedom of conduct and public expression," then the protection clause in Bill C-250 would have been a farce. The fact is that there is no judicial will to uphold or defend the rights of sincere Christians to voice historic Christian teaching on homosexuality.

The record of judicial activism has sown deep suspicion in the hearts and minds of reasonable people. The bottom line is that in Canada, religious rights are relative, while the rights of homosexuals are absolute.
Bill C-250, or whatever will be proposed to replace it, will exacerbate this situation because it will give activist judges the legal billy club to accuse Christians of hate crime. The evidence is there for anyone to read. Left wing, activist, God-hating judges who want to erase the Christian heritage

of this nation have been itching to criminalize Christian debate, speech, writing and text, and any expressed opinion about the (negative) moral dimensions of homosexuality. Hate crime legislation will be the tool they'll use to achieve this goal. Outrageous as it may seem, they are on the verge of getting away with it!

CHRISTOPHOBIA

8 | The Rationale For Hate Crime Legislation

Carnal man's problem is not a lack of evidence, reason or logic. The reality of God is everywhere before him. Man's problem is ethics. Man in his natural state hates God and God's plan of redemption. Man hates Christ, although he doesn't always admit it. – **Rev. Tristan Emmanuel**

Bill C-250, as we have demonstrated, was ill-conceived legislation. Its flaws were so numerous and so obvious that its progress in parliament was really mind-boggling. If not for Jean Chretien's precipitous decision to prorogue parliament on November 13, 2003, Bill C-250 would likely be the law of the land today. By the time you read this, it is possible, indeed very likely, that a replacement bill will be worming its way through the system. Not just in Canada, though. This is also a real threat in the United States. This begs the question: why are politicians so eager to consider laws of this nature? You know, the only conceivable answer I can come up with is "Christophobia".

This may sound ridiculous. After all, what is "Christophobia" anyway? Perhaps you have a sense of the word, but find it a little juvenile. Believe me, Christophobia isn't an adolescent attempt to play their game. It's not intended as a clever counterpoint to the term "homophobia", although I must admit it gives me some satisfaction. But Christophobia is not name-calling. It is a theological term I coined several years ago to describe thoughtless and irrational reactions to Christians, Christianity, and Christian teaching. The term came to me after I read several letters to the editor in my local newspaper that were so hysterical I realized many critics of Christianity have lost all sense of proportion.

I'm not simply talking about name-calling. Who hasn't experienced that? Christians certainly have not cornered the ridicule market, but we do get more than our fair share. You have heard them all, no doubt— "Jesus freaks", "Bible bashers" or "Holy rollers." No, I'm referring to *ad hominem* attacks (arguments that attack the *person* instead of the *message*) that illustrate how irrational many critics of Christianity really are. For example, when Christians steadfastly express historic Christian teaching on homosexuality, opponents attack our character. We are called "bigots," "homophobes," and "intolerant" because we have the nerve to believe in *absolutes*. It is this kind of character assassination that reveals the true nature of our critics. Ignorance is not the only problem. The offence is much more serious and deliberate.

This kind of criticism should not surprise us. Our post-modern culture, to the extent that it still has any philosophical basis, is "humanistic". The core ethic of humanism is relativism, which preaches that there are no absolute rules and no absolute morality. All morality is situational and based on personal likes and dislikes. In other words, the only real "absolute" in this ethic is that there "are no absolutes." Now, how often have you heard a Christian accuse a humanist of "bigotry" or "intolerance" because the humanist held sincerely to his or her belief in relativism? But when Christians enter the debate with an appeal to absolute truth or values, or even the notion of "moral good", a flurry of letters ensues, rife with sanctimonious criticism and accusations of bigotry, hate mongering, etc. It is character assassination, plain and simple.

Why? Because in expressing our belief in absolutes, we show ourselves to be "intolerant" to the secular mindset which believes that everything is relative. The trouble with relativism is that it is so incredibly hypocritical. If relativists really believed what they were preaching, they'd simply say, "You have your faith, I have mine. Who cares?" But they don't do that, do they? They obviously don't believe in "absolute relativism," because some things are less relative than others. Christianity is absolutely not relative to a Christophobic mindset.

But what does all this have to do with Canada's federal politicians? Or those in America for that matter? How did "Christophobia" help Bill C-250? Well, I'm sure that some of our national politicians are guilty of everything I've outlined. Many of them have an irrational revulsion to Christianity. Canadian readers will remember Stockwell Day. [12] He was vilified by his fellow politicians and some national columnists precisely because he dared to proclaim, publicly, that he was a born again Christian. Also, he insisted on taking Sundays off from the election campaign

- "Stockwell Day's just a crudely homophobic, Bible-thumping fundamentalist Neanderthal." *Mark Steyn commenting on " what people are saying."*

- "Blocwell Day." *Prime Minister Jean Chretien.*

- "As more people get to know Stockwell Day...they will find a leader who a lot of Canadians will find scary." *Progressive Conservative leader Joe Clark.*

- "Day believes the Flintstones is a documentary." *Warren Kinsella, Liberal organizer, commenting on Day's belief in Creationism.*

None of this should surprise us. The Bible says that the world despises Christians because it despises Christ.

- *And the light shines in the darkness, and the darkness did not comprehend it.* (John 1:5)

- *That was the true Light which gives light to every man coming into the world. He was in the world, and the world was made through Him, and the world did not know Him. He came to His own, and His own did not receive Him.* (John 1:9-12)

- *But the natural man does not receive the things of the Spirit of God, for they are foolishness to him; nor can he know them, because they are spiritually discerned.* (1 Cor. 2:14)

- *This I say, therefore, and testify in the Lord, that you should no longer walk as the rest of the Gentiles walk, in the futility of their mind, having their understanding darkened, being alienated from the life of God, because of the ignorance that is in them, because of the hardening of their heart; who, being past feeling, have given themselves over to lewdness, to work all uncleanness with greediness.* (Eph. 4:17-20)

- *Remember the word that I said to you, "A servant is not greater than his master.' If they persecuted Me, they will also persecute you.* (John 15:20)

It is sad but true. People, who reject Christians because of our faith, do so out of a blind revulsion to Christ. They are irrational in their rejection of Christ. It is their spiritual disorientation that drives their Christophobia.

But there is another more pragmatic side to Christophobia. Some politicians (and it is important that I stress some) are more concerned with getting re-elected, and maintaining appearances. The notion of getting re-elected, more than statecraft, is what drives some politicians. I will grant that this is a stereotype, but I believe it's valid. If you scratch these politicians deeply enough you'll find a man or woman running for re-election. Maintaining appearances, for these politicians, is an essential part of that process.

Now look at this politician and remember what we identified above. The overriding moral ethic, the national creed in North America at the start of the 21st Century, stemming from humanism and relativism, is "tolerance". This means that most politicians, in order to maintain appearances, have to appear to be "tolerant". If the national media, or even if a politician's local weekly newspaper for that matter, pegs that person as "intolerant," it is game over. Look at what happened to Stockwell Day.

Now, put it all together. Why did Bill C-250, a very ill conceived and poorly written law advance as far as it did? Quite simply, it's because politicians worry more about being labeled "homophobic" than "Christophobic." Politicians are afraid of being viewed as intolerant or unsympathetic to "gay" causes. The media did a stellar job of portraying Bill C-250 as a matter of "human rights", and politicians were subsequently led to believe that homosexuals needed the "protection" that the Bill would supposedly afford. No politician wants to be seen as being against anyone's "rights," especially "gay rights." No politician wants to be seen as opposing protection for those in society who are thought to be disadvantaged. It's not hard to see why Bill C-250 progressed so far. Whether a politician was specifically and theologically Christophobic didn't really matter. Supporting the gospel is politically more dangerous than supporting homosexual rights. Those who do the latter, however, illustrate Christ's point in Matt. 12:30: "He who is not for me is against me."

CHRISTOPHOBIA

A Conspiracy Or A Cultural Revolution

What is amazing about the advancement of the homosexual agenda in North American society, both in government and in the mainstream media, is that it has been the handiwork of a relatively small number of people. This advance proves the point that you don't need a majority of people to change a culture. A few dedicated activists organized and virtually re-ordered Canadian culture in less than one generation. This was done with the tacit cooperation of a poorly educated population that no longer knew how to think, discern, or be "discriminating" in the marketplace of ideas.

Svend Robinson and people like him have accomplished more than anyone, including themselves, thought possible. It didn't hurt that the group which engineered this juggernaut, this cultural coup d'etat, was made up largely of professionals and people who are well placed within society. Many wield considerable influence in all the relevant culture transforming institutions. Some, like Svend Robinson, are politicians. Others are judges, lawyers, and journalists. Starting in the late 1960s, this loosely defined group of activists set out to reshape Canadian society and destroy every conceivable social taboo as a matter of public justice—under the guise of "gay rights".

Back in 1971 they demanded:

1) The decriminalizing of sodomy, [13]
2) The removal of terms like "gross indecency" and "indecent act" from the Criminal Code of Canada, [14]
3) The redefinition of the term "in private," to mean "a condition of privacy," in the Criminal Code of Canada, [15]
4) The removal of "gross indecency" and "buggery" as grounds for indictment as a dangerous sexual offender,
5) Uniform age of consent laws for all female and male homosexual and heterosexual acts, [16]

6) An amendment to the Immigration Act to omit all references to homosexuals and "homosexualism," [17]

7) The right of equal employment and the promotion at all government levels for homosexuals, [18]

8) An amendment to the Divorce Act to omit "sodomy" and "homosexual acts" as grounds for divorce,

9) Equal rights for homosexuals in child custody cases,

10) The right of homosexuals to serve in the Armed Forces, [19]

11) The removal of provisions to convict service personnel of conduct unbecoming a service personnel,

12) The removal of policy statements that reflect negatively on homosexuals in government jobs,

13) All legal rights which currently exist for heterosexuals including:
    a. Filing joint income tax returns,
    b. Conferring pension rights,
    c. Public housing,
    d. Adoption rights,
    e. Right of free assembly and freedom of police harassment.

They got almost everything, one way or another, except two remaining areas:

1) "Same-sex marriage," or rather homosexual "marriage" and,

2) Hate-crime legislation that criminalizes all derogatory, discriminatory and moral criticism of homosexuality.

It is simply astounding that so few people have accomplished so many things in so little time. What has been even worse, much worse, than the advancement of this agenda has been the numbing silence of the Church throughout this period. It is absolutely inconceivable, when you think about it, that so few have been able to change so much with so little resistance from people whom Christ commanded to be "salt and light."

CHRISTOPHOBIA

What have we been doing? How is it possible that we've allowed our Judeo-Christian social ethic, our Criminal Code, Immigration Act, the Divorce Act, policy standards in the military, even human-rights definitions, to be completely rewritten? What were we Christians doing, or rather not doing? It is with some shame that I admit that I, too, share equally in our complacency and apathy.

As I've been traveling around and speaking to churches I'm often asked this question. "How could it have gone so far?" The only answer is that we have *allowed* it. The *church* is responsible. Now that the dikes of our culture have been blown wide open and the floodwaters of immorality are pouring in, we're finding it incredibly difficult to stem the flow. Outside of a complete cultural transformation and reformation, it will now take an act of God to stop this tide. The church, in all of its denominational and broken manifestations, will have to start taking the Lordship of Christ seriously and begin to disciple our nation. But I'm getting ahead of myself here.

There is another aspect to all this which is worth mentioning, and it indirectly highlights the systemic nature of Christophobia. If a few Christians had decided back in the late 1960s to reshape Canada, or at least to try to exercise enough influence over high-ranking officials in government to make a difference, our critics would be screaming "conspiracy" from the rooftops at this very hour.

We would be hearing an endless diatribe about the intentions of Christians. The self-righteous secularists would be wagging their fingers and telling us we "don't have the right to impose our morality." We'd be pelted with the trite secular slogan: "Separation of Church and State!" or "Inquisition? Never again." All because the humanists and homosexual activists fear that if Christians came to power we'd see a repeat of past sins. I can hear it already: *"They're trying to create a theocracy!"* (the notion of Church control of the state).

The Real Reason Behind Hate Crime Legislation

But this is really quite laughable. Most Christians are as opposed to theocracy as most homosexual activists. This is partly because Christians really don't understand what a theocracy is, and in that sense the fear is misplaced. But it is mostly because Christians generally do believe in the institutional separation of Church and State (which is far different than the separation of faith from public policy, the position the secularists have wrongly sought to impose). Moreover, no Christian wants to return to the days of the Inquisition. We *do* believe in privacy laws. And we do *not* believe that the state should be used as a secret service to entrap anyone for "sins" committed in the privacy of their home.

But when viewed objectively, the concerns that secularists and homosexuals have with Christian involvement in the public square are really off the wall. It is sheer hypocrisy. If anyone is guilty of "imposing" their worldviews on society, it has not been the Christians. Homosexual activists, who would scream at the first sign that Christians might be *influencing* government, have been doing precisely that, working to impose *their* morality on the rest of the country. While expressing grave concerns over the motives of those they see as trying to create a "theocracy", they have in effect created a "homocracy" where their views of morality have taken over the public square. In some sense, this "homocracy" really is nothing more than another version of theocracy, where society will soon be forced to bow before the triune gods of "tolerance", "human rights", and "sexual orientation."

But lest I paint them all with the same brush, some homosexuals are equally opposed to the idea of this "homocracy." John Keller, president of Homosexuals Opposed to Pride Extremism (HOPE), is one of them. He is deeply troubled by the homosexual lobby in Canada. He publicly stated at a REAL Women conference in March 2003:

> *Believe me, my life would be much simpler if I didn't have to contend with all of this. But how can I sit still when my public image is*

embarrassingly represented by a small but vociferous clique of radicals bent on making the whole world their closet? How can I sit still when the main stream media constantly gives unequivocal support to the lies, myths, distortions and propaganda of modern gay activists? How can I sit still when my freedoms are being threatened and the traditions and institutions of my country are being compromised?

Who would have thought a homosexual would share some of the concerns raised in this book? John Keller's statement points out that it is truly a select group that is pushing "gay rights." Homosexual activists don't speak for all homosexuals. Mr. Keller makes this point abundantly clear.

So I formed HOPE (Homosexuals Opposed to Pride Extremism) to give a voice to gays and lesbians who choose to live with dignity and discretion; who don't wake up every day looking for discrimination under the bed, and who don't go running to the governments, the courts, or the human rights commissions for a lifetime of therapeutic preferences.

The honorable Senator Anne Cools also believes that a group of "elite activists" are behind the push for hate crime law and other so-called "protections".

Bill C-250 is directed at those Canadians whose moral opinions are unwanted by an elite group of homosexual rights activists, a group that is well connected to the government and those who seek to overwhelm their opponents and to impose their moral views on them. This elite disagrees morally with millions of Canadians. Not content merely to disagree with them and to co-exist with them, this elite, by Bill C-250, seeks to persecute and to prosecute them criminally. [20]

This group historically was not able to champion its cause openly in the marketplace of ideas. More recently, however, society has become more and more accommodating to its agenda. Nevertheless, to get this far this group has furtively influenced society through the back doors of government. That means these people have been working to impose, not convince.

Am I saying there's a conspiracy behind this? No. If this were a conspiracy it would suggest that those in power (i.e. Canada's federal Liberals) are innocent because they were duped or tricked. But they were not. Neither government, nor society in general was duped. There is an implicit, if not explicit, political acceptance of homosexual rights at every level of government. In the broader culture it is even worse. A general mindset, an attitude, has evolved as a result of factors that have been influencing the culture for years. The arts, entertainment, and media are big influences, with media perhaps the most influential. Those in the media shape public opinion and public morality. The more we are exposed to homosexuality as "normal", the more we see homosexuals portrayed as just "ordinary people", the more accommodating everyone becomes. Once society and culture start accommodating and even defending some positions and views that were previously considered immoral or at least "wrong", the dike is broken. What was once a taboo is now "mainstream," and it is almost impossible to return to the previous moral standards.

In addition to the cultural influences, there is another, more coercive and sinister agenda being promoted behind the scenes by a number of homosexual activists. These activists have used what HOPE's John Keller calls "Stalinist" tactics to influence, intimidate, and impose. Once again, they succeed because most people fear being labeled a right-wing Christian zealot, or a "homophobe," far more than they worry about being called a "homophile" or, as I prefer a Christophobe.

CHRISTOPHOBIA

Avenging Traditional Morality

I predict Christophobia will get worse before it gets better. Soon it will no longer be just a way to marginalize Christians. Homosexual activists are intent on using laws like Bill C-250 to criminalize all moral disapproval of their sin. Christophobia will soon become legal practice of civil government.

Senator Cools makes this very clear. In a late night session of the Senate of Canada, she passionately appealed to the Senators saying:

> *Honorable senators should grasp the enormity and danger of the proposal before us. Senators should understand its goal and should unmask it for the menace that it is. The measure is humanely couched and articulated in terms of equality, but it is a cruel proposition intended to criminalize the verbal and written expression of moral opinion on human sexuality and on human sexual practices.*

While she does not directly associate Bill C-250 with the silencing of the gospel, she does correctly argue that Bill C-250 will criminalize moral disapproval of homosexuality.

In her speech, Senator Cools indicated that human sexuality, practice, and lust have fallen under moral judgment from time immemorial. There has never been a time or a culture that has not assumed the right to judge human sexuality, especially homosexuality.

But homosexual activists have disdain for history and tradition, because history and tradition have not favored them. In the West, until fairly recent times, the Church played the single greatest role in shaping the moral philosophy of society. Western jurisprudence suppressed homosexual behavior because it was seen to be bad for society. Hate crime laws would provide the homosexual community with some measure of revenge by placing a gag order on moral disapproval, and ultimately on the gospel.

Of course, our opposition to homosexual marriage or hate crime law doesn't stem from "traditionalism". That would be like saying something is right just because it has been this way in the past. But just because something "has been," doesn't necessarily make it right. Dr. Jeffrey Satinover, past president of the C.G. Jung Foundation, a group noted for its work on psychotherapy, has said that " ...it is conceivable that we may be holding on to... opinions... which are in fact mistaken, but the burden of proof rests with those who would alter such traditions."

In other words, just because homosexual activists are promoting their lifestyle as an "orientation" that is worthy of societal approval, doesn't necessarily mean they are right. They must either prove homosexuality is genetically determined and therefore inescapable, or they must prove that it is somehow morally and socially "noble" to be gay. But homosexual activists have done neither. [21] That is why the introduction of laws like Bill C-250 is such an outrage. Homosexual activists have dogmatically and *arbitrarily* assumed the moral certitude of their position on "orientation," and are now demanding that all moral disapproval of this position be made illegal.

As Senator Cools argues, homosexual activists arrogantly propose to elevate sexual behavior and practice to the status of an immutable (unchangeable) characteristic, like a person's skin color, and they want use the *Criminal Code of Canada* to retaliate against those who disapprove of homosexuality on moral grounds.

Now, here is where it gets dicey. It is the Senator's stated and solemn opinion that a law like Bill C-250 will be used not simply as a measure to protect homosexuals but also to *oppress average people of faith.*

CHRISTOPHOBIA

Bill C-250 is about forming and building a legal base from which modern inquisitions of persons for their moral beliefs, values, ideas, standards and moral opinions will ensue.

The honorable Senator is bang on. It is not just pastors who could get into trouble with the law. It is also the average Christian who could face serious legal sanctions. That is why I earlier referred to this kind of legislation as a legal billy club. It is legalized Christophobia. Bill C-250 was precisely the kind of law that homosexual activists, politicians, and judges had been looking for. It is a weapon to wage judicial war against all those who oppose the homosexual lifestyle on moral grounds. Let there be no mistake. Its intended target was Christians.

The Good News Of Redemption Requires Admission Of Sin

"Okay, so we won't be able to tell homosexuals their behavior is wrong, so what? I still don't see why I can't share the love of Jesus with them. Surely sharing the message of God's love won't get me into trouble. Besides, you're making it sound like we should all be activists and speak out on social policies." Sadly, this is how many Christians will respond to the message of this book. Contemporary Christianity is caught up with sentimental, easy-believism, and nothing makes this clearer than when we knowingly or unwittingly compromise the message of the gospel by neglecting to tell the whole story.

"But the gospel is good news. How could that be criminal?" Good point. Yes, the gospel is good news. In fact, that is exactly what the word means: good news. But it is only good news to those who accept it as good news. They can only accept it if they first understand the bad news. It is precisely here where the problem lies. You can't tell the good news if you first don't tell people, including homosexuals, the bad news.

The Real Reason Behind Hate Crime Legislation

I remember reading a car decal that poked fun at the slogan: "Jesus is the Answer." It smugly asked: "What is the Question?" I'm sure the intent of the bumper sticker bordered on the blasphemous. But the point is worth considering. Far too many Christians don't want to talk about the context that surrounds the gospel. They don't want to talk about the "bad news".

In other words they don't want to talk about sin. If you don't talk about sin, then the fact that Jesus is the answer makes no sense at all. First we need to establish the reality of sin (the bad news), and that everyone is a sinner, and then the good news will start to make sense.

The gospel outlines why people need Jesus, why "Jesus is the answer". And you know, after several years in the gospel ministry, if there is anything I have become more convinced of (next to the dangers of Bill C-250), it is this: everybody needs Jesus, including homosexuals. People may not want Jesus. That is an entirely different issue. They may not want Him because it means giving up sin, giving up autonomy, or giving up homosexuality. But they need Him. They need Him more than they can know.

They need Him precisely because of the bad news. The bad news is that man is alienated from God. Man is lost. Man is sinful. Man is under God's wrath and judgment. Right now, all those who remain outside of Christ, and that could include your neighbor, a fellow worker, your Member of Parliament or Congressman, and the homosexual, or anyone you may know, all these people who don't have a relationship with Jesus are under the wrath of God and await His eternal judgment. (Rom. 1:18, Col. 1:19-22) All of this is very bad news. That is why the gospel is good news.

But it is not enough to talk about sin in general. Sin is a concept that most people find completely foreign. People can relate to "mistakes," or "bad deeds," and in some cases they can even relate to "evil". Everyone instinctively understands that mass murderers or certain deviant criminals like Paul Bernardo are "evil". [22] But specific sin is a different matter completely. It is off the radar screen because sin is a spiritual concept. The carnal mind can't relate.

Sin is so unreal. Talking about sin is considered oppressive and judgmental and intolerant. It is said that "sin" is something the Church created to oppress the masses and extort large sums of money out of the witless. "What do you mean I'm a sinner?"

When dealing with lost people, we need to be able to drive home the point, lovingly yet firmly, that regardless of the past sins of *the Church*, they are a sinner *today* in the eyes of God. A lot of people, if you raise the notion of God with them, will tell you, "God? I don't have a problem with God at all." But what they don't realize is that God has a problem with them. That problem is their sin. We need to point out to them how sin is evident in their life. Herein lies the rub on the issue of homosexuality, just as it does with all other sins. The minute we start pointing to specific sins, people think we are attacking them on a personal level. In reality, we are not doing this at all. We are actually trying to help. But to the carnal mind it feels like an attack. Remember Joe Clark's comment about Stockwell Day? "....a leader who a lot of Canadians will find scary"? Scary indeed. People are afraid of being convicted.

The exercise of evangelism, presenting people with the Gospel, is difficult enough in the present climate. When you add to this difficulty the reality of hate crime legislation and the possibility of criminal charges, you begin to see how these laws are an impediment to the gospel.

Hate crime law, and the philosophies that surround it, teach people that as far as the law is concerned, homosexuality is not a sin. It sends the message that calling homosexuality a sin is equivalent to genocidal hate-speech. But the Bible doesn't just talk about homosexuality being immoral. At the core of the Gospel is the notion that homosexuals, just like all sinners, are in need of a Savior. This Gospel, if applied to the heart by the Holy Spirit, will cause homosexuals, as it will cause *all sinners*, to loathe themselves, to feel remorse, and to repent. This is what constitutes "hate" to them. It is "hateful" to suggest that homosexuality is a sin. It is hateful to suggest that someone's "orientation" is alterable, or that he/she has *chosen* to be homosexual. To those who advocate hate crime legislation, this notion is just as hateful as suggesting that someone's skin color is a sin.

Let me put this into a real life situation. Imagine a gospel service where a pastor gives a full-orbed gospel message. Imagine that one of those in the audience happens to be a homosexual, and he has just heard the pastor preach on 1 Cor. 6:9-10 which states:

> *Do you not know that the unrighteous will not inherit the kingdom of God? Do not be deceived. Neither fornicators, nor idolaters, nor adulterers, nor homosexuals, nor sodomites, nor thieves, nor covetous, nor drunkards, nor revilers, nor extortioners will inherit the kingdom of God.*

He just heard the pastor give the bad news. He heard the pastor speak about sexual immorality. He heard that two of those sins are directly related to homosexuality. He heard the pastor point out that those guilty of these sins cannot inherit the "kingdom of God." But the pastor didn't leave it there. He took him, and everyone else in the congregation, to the next verse, which lays out the plan of redemption. The pastor has told them all that there is hope if they want it. In Christ anyone guilty of these sins can find salvation.

Now, to Christians, this sounds very loving and positive. But imagine what it might sound like to a homosexual who isn't interested in changing. Imagine how completely enraged he would be at the suggestion that his "orientation" is a sin. Imagine how completely outraged he would be at the suggestion that he is disqualified from heaven because of his "orientation." Imagine, also, how completely beside himself he would be because the pastor had the nerve to suggest that if he "turns to Christ," he can leave the life he presently loves.

If a law such as Bill C-250 were to pass, what might this man do? He could walk out and never return to that church. But he also could pursue legal action against the church and the minister because, under the definition of hate-propaganda, the entire service created "an environment in which his dignity was affronted on the basis of his sexual orientation." He might consider that he was subjected to "hate-speech leading to the condition of sexual genocide."

Does this mean that we should stop preaching the gospel to homosexuals to avoid legal attacks? No, of course not. That's not my point. My point is simply to illustrate, as clearly as possible, that the gospel is the ultimate target of laws like Bill C-250. It may be that homosexuals don't necessarily see this, but it is the case. The gospel is the target of the attack. It always was and it always will be.

When Jesus preached the gospel, he came into legal conflict with the Pharisees. When Stephen preached the gospel of Jesus, he was confronted with legal opposition from the Sanhedrin. When John preached the gospel, the Romans jailed him on the island of Patmos. (Rev. 1:9) When Peter preached the gospel, Nero executed him. When Paul preached the gospel, the Jews persecuted him. They even used the Roman courts to advance the persecution. (Acts 17:7; 18:12-13.) Preaching the gospel effectively will lead to hostilities and legal attacks at some point. That is why I began by saying that Christians are called to be activists. Preaching the gospel of Jesus Christ, in the final analysis, is politically incorrect. (Acts 5:29) It goes against the grain of any political and legal order that refuses to acknowledge the kingship of Christ. This is why hate crime law is, ultimately, motivated by Christophobia. Such law seek to silence the Church.

9 | There Is No Quick Fix

The present chasm between the generations has been brought about almost entirely by a change in the concept of truth. Whenever you look today, the new concept holds the field. The consensus about us is almost monolithic, whether you review the arts, literature or simply read the newspaper and magazine such as Time, Life, Newsweek, The Listener or The Observer. On every side you can feel the stranglehold... **Francis Schaeffer.**

The advancement and wide scale cultural endorsement of homosexuality is a problem, a very serious problem. But in the final analysis it is not the problem. In my estimation, the "gay-friendly" society is the culmination of a problem that started a long time ago.

Western culture is collapsing. It is collapsing because it has been trying to rebuild itself on a post-modern quagmire. That quagmire is secular humanism. Secular humanism is a religion every bit as much as Christianity. It has a god: man. It has a temple: the state. It has a priesthood: activist judges, agnostic lawyers, and materialist scientists. It has an ethic: relative-feel-goodism. And it has laity: Joe-average citizen.

Since the rise of Darwinism in the mid-19th century, secular humanism has invaded every relevant cultural institution in the West. Civil government, courts, schools, media, and many churches have adopted a secular view of the world and have made disciples of the average person. This secular view became the new paradigm for looking at everything from science to politics. As theologian Herman Bavinck wrote at the dawn of the last century,

> (M)an has undertaken the gigantic effort of interpreting the whole world, and all things that are therein, in their origin, essence, and end... purely and strictly scientifically, that is, without God. [23]

But the advancement of secular humanism didn't just happen. Unwitting and sincere believing people of the past generations aided its advancement. These Christians believed that science had disproven the created origin of man, that reason and knowledge were antithetical to faith, and so, Bible-believing Christians shunned the unbelieving culture.

Culture came to belong to unbelievers, and social-gospelizers. Instead of endeavouring in society, in politics, law, media and the arts, pious believers focussed on more heavenly pursuits—missions, Bible study, prayer and the end-times. They paid a heavy price for abandoning society.

> A good man leaves an inheritance to his children's children. But the wealth of the sinner is stored up for the righteous. (Prov. 13:22)

Don't get me wrong. Missions, Bible study, prayer and waiting for Christ's return are not bad things. These are not bad ways for Christians to be spending their time. But it should never have been an either/or situation. Christians should have pursued cultural endeavours from a Christian perspective as vigorously as they did their church related projects. As it stands, the children, the precious inheritance from God, did the same: they placed a wedge between matters of faith and matters of culture. Secular humanistic thinking and worldview filled the vacuum that Christianity once occupied. As secularism grew more dominant, more and more Christians began to adopt secular views of culture.

Solution

Some of us believe that we will be safe in our distinctive denominations. We seem to cling to the crumbling façade that we have freedom of religion, and that this will be ours as an inherent right forever. Others have begun to wake up, and are starting to fight back. But the fight has focussed too much on politics. Too many Christians have believed that if we simply "recapture" Ottawa or Washington we'll rescue our respective nations. I don't believe that will work in either country.

Freedom of religion is an illusion. There is no "freedom" for the Christian religion. As long as Christians are willing to take a backseat to secularism, freedom of religion will remain an illusion. A culture can only endorse one dominant religion. In spite of what the so-called multiculturalists assert, there can be no peaceful coexistence between rival religions. But our problem is far more difficult. Too many Christians aren't prepared to engage in the cultural and religious battles that are currently under way. They want to live at peace, even if that is a peace at the expense of Christianity. And this is the only reason secularism continues to advance. Too many of us are content to keep our Christianity confined to personal acts of piety and "closet" worship.

Secular humanists don't object much to this kind of closeted Christianity. But, homosexual "marriage" could change all that. If homosexuals are allowed to marry, even our private houses of worship are open to their agenda. They want our clergy to marry them, even if we object to "homosexual" marriage. So much for peaceful co-existence.

More to the point, capturing the political enclaves won't work either (not that we shouldn't try). Why? Because if a culture remains unconverted, perverted and secular, it won't matter a hill of beans if we "capture" our political capitals. All that will do is create an environment of political revolution. Unconverted, secular citizens will revolt against a Christian ordering of government. Remember, as Christians we don't believe in imposing a culture from the top down.

What are we to do then? Is it wrong to be involved in politics? No. That's not what I'm suggesting. We should engage our present politicians. We should run for office because we are citizens of our countries with an equal right to the public square. But we must recognize that this is not enough. The problems faced by the societies in Canada and America are far too pervasive to be solved simply by recapturing Ottawa or Washington. Secular humanism affects every facet of our nations' identities. That is why only a responsible and comprehensive cultural solution will work. Christian culture is that solution. To be precise, a "bottom up" Christian culture is the solution.

Our cultures should be Christian—not by political coercion, but by cultural discipleship. We need to get back into all the relevant culture-shaping institutions and become the best in the field as Christians. That means that we should develop a self-conscious Christian world and life view and apply it to every sphere of cultural endeavour. Remember, Canada's culture, and America's too, for that matter, were explicitly Christian in their early days. Canada was Christian for nearly 100 years and America for nearly 300 years. This is what both should be today. This does not mean that a particular Church should dictate public policy. We don't believe a Church should rule the s tate. Neither does it mean that we should return to the "good old days." Believe me there were plenty of problems in our Christian cultures of the past.

But what it does mean is that we should forge ahead with the good principles of the past and seek better ways to apply them today. It also means that faith neither *can* nor *should* be separated from the public square. That means that Christians, *as Christians*, should lead culture rather than abandon it. Christians should lead as fathers, mothers, university students, businessmen, attorneys, pastors, judges, educators, journalists, artists, musicians, salesmen, technicians, physicians, clerks, janitors and yes, as politicians too.

I believe that only a Christian culture will guarantee the freedoms of everyone, including those who disagree with Christianity, because Christianity is rooted in divine truth, justice and love; because a Christian culture is built on a rock that will withstand cultural crisis. And yes, this will mean that certain lifestyles will not be endorsed, promoted or sanctioned, because certain lifestyles are inimical to a healthy and prosperous society.

Justification

What gives Christians the right to do this? Good question. As "salt and light" (Matt. 5:13-16), according to God's Word (Matt 4:4), and the power of the Holy Spirit (Jn. 16:12), we have been commissioned to make a disciple of our nations.

> *All authority has been given to Me in heaven and on earth. Go therefore and make disciples of all the nations, baptizing them in the name of the Father and of the Son and of the Holy Spirit, teaching them to observe all things that I have commanded you; and lo, I am with you always, even to the end of the age.* (Matt. 28:18-20)

Remember the discussion on Christ's sovereign authority, and how that authority determines what is and isn't a human right? Well, He has called us to disciple the nations. Discipling a nation includes discipling individuals in that nation. But individuals do not live in a vacuum. We are commissioned to disciple individuals in their social context: family, career, and community.

Moreover, we are called to disciple the whole nation, not just some in the nation. A nation is not simply a tribe of people, or even primarily a body politic. It is a collective of individuals bound by common custom and moulded by common cultural institutions: family, church, school, city council, regional/provincial/state and national (federal) governments, and the judiciary, to name only a few. We have been commissioned to disciple a nation, its culture and its cultural institutions.

Impossible? I admit it is a daunting task. Even overwhelming. That is precisely why it is called a "*Great* Commission." Whether we ultimately succeed, or whether this is the end of history is not the point. The point is that the King of kings has commissioned us, Jesus Christ, who has all authority in heaven and on earth. He has commanded it and that is all that matters. That is the point, and it seems to me that even if a few of us engage in this task, as a small minority, we have no reason to despair.

Let me repeat: if a few homosexual activists have been able to push their agenda this far even though they represent only two or three percent of the population, why can't we do the same? Our hope, our strength, our wisdom, and our source of courage to fulfil the Great Commission do not rest in us. We would not be discipling our nations in our own strength. Christ has promised that He will be with us always, even to the end of the age. What do homosexuals have that we don't? Sure, they have some judges, lawyers, and politicians, and they've even got big business on their side. But we've got the greatest advocate in the world: the Spirit of Truth. They've got civil governments and the United Nations empowering them. We have God Almighty. They have nothing on us. Go therefore and make a disciple of this culture—that is the only solution.

The Real Reason Behind Hate Crime Legislation

Endnotes

[1] All Scripture is quoted from the New King James Version.

[2] Some controversy surrounds the interpretation of this passage. Roman Catholic theologians cite this passage for the establishment of the papacy; that Peter, as the first Pope, was the rock upon which the church would be built. Protestants hold a different view based on Paul's discussion in Ephesians (2:20) of the church being built on the foundation of the apostles (plural). This discussion is not necessarily germane to my point. My point, rather, is that the passage promises that indeed the church "will prevail". Matthew Henry has a number of pertinent observations that illustrate my point:

1) Christ here promises to preserve and secure his church, when it is built. The gates of hell shall not prevail against it; neither against this truth, nor against the church which is built upon it.

   a. This implies that the church has enemies that fight against it ... The gates of hell are the powers and policies of the devil's kingdom, the dragon's head and horns, by which he makes war with the Lamb; all that comes out of hell gates, as being hatched and contrived there.

b. These fight against the church by opposing gospel truths, corrupting gospel ordinances, persecuting good ministers and good Christians;

c. Drawing or driving, persuading by craft or forcing by cruelty, to that which is inconsistent with the purity of religion; this is the design of the gates of hell, to root out the name of Christianity, (Ps. 83:4).

2) This assures us that the enemies of the church shall not gain their point.

a. While the world stands, Christ will have a church in it, in which his truths and ordinances shall be owned and kept up, in spite of all the opposition of the powers of darkness; They shall not prevail against it, (Ps. 129:1-2).

b. This gives no security to any particular church, or church-governors that they shall never err, never apostatize or be destroyed;

c. The church may be foiled in particular encounters, but in the main battle it shall come off more than a conqueror.

d. Particular believers are kept by the power of God, through faith, unto salvation, 1 Peter 1:5.

(Matthew Henry's *Commentary on the Whole Bible: New Modern Edition, Electronic Database*. Copyright (c) 1991 by Hendrickson Publishers, Inc.)

[3] Paul's argument about the purpose of government is directly related to Paul's previous comment forbidding "vigilantism." It is unlawful for Christians to take the law into their own hands and avenge themselves (as it is for everyone). God will have vengeance on the "evil doer," the criminal – "vengeance is mine saith the Lord." Paul's point is that government, even unbelieving government, serves God's divine purpose because it is a minister of God, serving the interests of divine justice.

[4] Don Wall, "Editor's Desk," *Forever Young*, Hamilton/Niagara, August

2003.

5   Marshall K. Kirk and Phil Erastes, "The Overhauling of Straight America," *Guide*, November 1987.

6   Quoted in *"Massachusetts News"* (www.massnews.com). May 9, 2001. "Dr. Spitzer Says Homosexuals Can Change."

7   Dr. Robert Spitzer, *Narth Release* (National Association for Research & Therapy of Homosexuality), "Prominent Psychiatrist Announces New Study Results: Some Gays CAN Change." May 9, 2001.

8   Bruce Rind, Ph.D., Robert Bauserman, Ph.D., and Phillip Tromovitch, Ph.D., "An Examination of Assumed Properties Based on Non-Clinical Samples," presented at the Paulus Kirk, Rotterdam, the Netherlands, December 18, 1998.

9   "Homosexual Activists Work to Lower the Age of Sexual Consent," citing Enrique T. Rueda, *The Homosexual Network*, Connecticut: The Devin Adair Company, 1982, p. 201.

10   Michael Alhonte, "The Politics of Ageism: A Statement to the Lesbian and Gay Community," www.nambla1.de

11   Mark Gevisser and Edwin Cameron, Defiant Desire: *Gay and Lesbian Lives in South Africa*, Ravan Press, Johannesburg, South Africa, 1994.

12   A Christian man who served first in the Alberta provincial legislature and then switched to federal politics and became the first leader of the Canadian Alliance Party, and the Leader of the Official Opposition.

13   Pierre Trudeau, who as minister of Justice in 1969 reformed the Criminal Code of Canada to decriminalize sodomy, declared in 1967, "The state has no place in the bedrooms of the nation."

14   "What We Demanded: What We Got," Canadian Lesbian & Gay Archives, www.clga.ca, April 21, 1998. "The 1969 amendments to the Criminal Code had been part of an 'omnibus'" bill, included legal reforms not only on sex offences but on matters as wide ranging as abortion, contraception, gambling, lotteries, and gun control...as early as 1974, the Law Reform Commission of Canada recommended that all but the most serious offences be removed from the Criminal Code... in a Nov 1978

report, saying laws prohibiting buggery, bestiality, gross indecency, indecent assault, and rape should be replaced by only two provisions: 'sexual interference' and 'sexual aggression.'"

[15] Ibid., "In private...the involvement or presence of more than two persons no longer automatically defines an act as not 'private'" in the Criminal Code of Canada.

[16] Ibid., "in early 1985... they called for a uniform age of consent (16 for most sexual acts; 18 for anal and vaginal penetration) and some other progressive reforms." But by 1995, "it was set at 14 for all sexual acts except anal intercourse. It can be as low as 12 if an older person is within two years of the younger person's age and is not in a position of authority over the younger person."

[17] Ibid., "Demand met, six years and seven months after it was made (in 1971)."

[18] Ibid., "The goal of this demand in 1971 was not simply to achieve employment rights, but to challenge the usual rationale for withholding them: 'national security.' Homosexuals were considered susceptible to blackmail and thus an automatic security risk." By 1996 homosexuals were employed by the Canadian Armed forces and the RCMP as open homosexuals.

[19] Ibid., "[on] Oct 27, 1992, in a settlement with lesbian Michelle Douglas who had challenged her 1988 dismissal, Michelle Douglas got $100,000; the Forces got a court order forcing them to concede that their anti-gay practices violated the Charter and would stop forthwith. A statement issued by the Chief of Defense Staff the same day said: 'Canadians, regardless of their sexual orientation, will now be able to serve their country in the Canadian Forces without restriction.'"

[20] Anne C. Cools, speech on the second reading of Bill C-250, to amend the Criminal Code (hate propaganda), Debates of the Senate, 2nd Session, 37th Parliament, Volume 140, Number 89, Monday, October 27, 2003.

[21] Dr. Jeffrey Satinover, psychiatrist, authority on the research related to homosexuality, and past president of the C.G. Jung Foundation, in a speech to the Family Research Council ("Capitol Hill Briefing on the Defense of

Marriage Act," July 2, 1996). Dr. Satinover said that "three different kinds of studies that have been put forth largely by the media, as demonstrating the fact—the supposed fact—that homosexuality is innate, genetic, and unchangeable" have proven the opposite of what has been touted. Based on the scientific evidence homosexuality is not innate, genetic and unchangeable.

[22] On September 1, 1995 Paul Bernardo was convicted of first-degree murder in the sex slayings of two teen-age girls in southern Ontario. He was also found guilty of kidnapping, forcible confinement, aggravated sexual assault and committing an indignity to a body. He was sentenced to life in prison without parole.

[23] Herman Bavinck, in the *Methodist Review,* November 1901.

Printed in the United States
31091LVS00005B/82-99